Hal o' the Heath:

The Wandering Heir.

By E. H. BURRAGE.

SPLENDIDLY ILLUSTRATED.

Hal o' the Heath

THE WANDERING HEIR.

CHAPTER I.

THE LONELY SPORTSMAN OF THE MOOR—A WARNING.

A FEW years ago—the precise number does not signify—there lived on a lonely moor in the south of England the strangest hermit the world had ever seen.

He was a hermit in one sense, but not in another, for, although he shut himself out from the world, he had one companion, and in addition he was young, handsome—with the high bearing that spoke of birth and breeding.

No cave was his home, but a small cottage right away in the heart of the moor.

All his needs were obtained from a town a few miles off by the grim attendant, who went thither once a-week.

People crossed the moor by well-known paths, and at wide intervals there were cottages in which dwelt some folks engaged in humble occupations ; but with none of these did the young hermit or attendant hold communion.

In passing the young recluse would give the people Good-day, and perchance bestow a coin upon the poorest but that was all.

He had given no name, nor his man either ; but the people had bestowed upon the younger man the name of Hal o' the Heath, for one man had overheard the servant address his superior as Master Hal.

Once, in the market-place, the man had been asked what his name was.

"Grip!" he replied, curtly.

And as Grip was he known thenceforward.

For two years master and man had resided on the heath, and no living creature came to visit them; but every now and then Grip would call at the town post-office for letters.

He received very few, and they were addressed simply to "Hal."

Two amusements Hal o' the Heath was known to indulge in—reading and shooting.

Sometimes he could be seen wandering about book in hand, at other times with his gun; and it was said of him that he was a "dead sure shot."

"He never misses," said the people. "He sights his bird or hare, touches the trigger, and it is dead."

That he had a right to shoot over the moor was certain, for what he did was never questioned; but how he acquired it nobody knew.

All they did know was that it belonged to old Lord Ferrus, who had long been past the use of the gun, and lived in one of his big houses far away north.

The moor, it may be said, ran right down to the sea, from which it was divided by a line of rugged rocks.

It was a lonely, desolate shore, where no fisherman's boat or cot could be seen.

There was another strange occupant of the moor—a woman, and her home was by the sea.

It was only a few sticks roughly thatched, standing in a sheltered nook.

She was an old, weird woman, very like a witch, and the people said she was one. She lived in a semi-savage way, sometimes hobbling into the town to get a few necessaries.

It took her a day and night to perform the journey, but she was never known to sleep away from home.

Old Margery they called her, and how old she was they could only guess. The simple folk shunned her, and she took a grim delight in the terror she evidently inspired in their bosoms.

It was said that years and years ago she had been found after a storm sitting on the beach beside a dead man, holding his head in her lap and weeping bitterly.

Hard by was a small upturned boat, cast ashore by the angry waves.

The story went that they were a handsome pair, and that she refused all help to bury him, but performed that office with her own hands, laying him down in a hole in the sand out of the reach of storm and tide in the sheltered spot where she had dwelt so many years.

In Hal o' the Heath she took a great interest, and had been seen watching him as he strode across the moor ; but, as far as the few curious watchers could see, they did not exchange a word.

Whether they did or not, a day came when they did speak, and to some purpose, as our story shall unfold.

It was one morning in the middle of September, when Hal was out with his gun, and the pursuit of game led him down close to the sea.

He was alone, for Grip had gone away to the town on one of his excursions.

As he came near the sea he stopped to rest, to look about him, first at the restless waves, and then at the cloud-speckled sky.

Then, from behind a rock, slowly uprose the form of Old Margery, and extending her long, thin arm towards him, she cried—

" Hal o' the Heath, a word with you !"

He was not startled, but surprised. Drawing himself up a little stiffly, he said, in a quiet tone—

"Well, dame, what have you to say to me ?"

"Why do you hide here ?" she asked ; " you with youth and strength and all the gifts that should make a peerless man of you ? Is there no better place than this deserted heath for such as you ?"

A flush spread over his face, and he did not immediately answer her. She waited, with her arm extended still, for him to speak.

" Might I not as well ask why *you* are here ?" he said ;

"what has kept you for half a century away rom the world?"

"Scorn," she said.

"Ah! well," he answered, "perhaps it is scorn that keeps me here, too?"

"Scorn and — SHAME!" she said. "Nay, start not and frown at me! There is no stain on *you*, but on those who bear your name. You fret alone in the stillness of the night over the lost honour of a noble name. But will that help you? Will it stop the downward rush of the brother you love?"

"Who has been talking to you?" cried Hal. "Is it Grip? Nay, not him. Why have you been prying into my affairs, you beldame?"

"A beldame now,' she said, with a sudden softening in her voice, "but not always so. What was the world to me when I had lost ALL? Was I the woman to carry my broken heart into the vain, frivolous, heartless world?"

"Forgive me!" he said. "I did not mean to pain you."

"Enough!" she returned; "let all that concerns me go. It is of you I would speak. See there!"

She made a sweeping motion of her arm away to the left, and following the action, he saw in the distance a man wearing a long cloak, and with his hat drawn over his eyes, standing on a rock.

The moment he perceived he was seen he leaped down from the rock into a little hollow behind and vanished.

"Do you know him?" she asked.

"No," replied Hal. "Possibly it is some tourist, wandering here to get a rest from the turmoil of the world?"

"He is the foe of your house," said Old Margery. "He has come here to tell you that on this earth there is now no home you can call your own. No; not even that shepherd's cot where you have dwelt for two weary years.'

"Who said they were weary years? Not I, by my life."

"No, but they have been weary," said old Margery. "The only tie you have on earth broken—you know it—with a cloud of dishonour on your head, where should you, with your high sense of truth and honour, rest?"

"Enough of this," said Hal, impatiently. "What mummery is it? Do you want to tell me my fortune—to read my future?"

"Stay!" she cried.

Hobbling down from her elevated perch she came slowly up to him.

"Give me your hand," she said. "Oh! it is no mummery. I do not ask you to cross mine with gold or silver—I ask nothing but patience and a belief in my unselfish interest in you."

He was amazed and a little awed.

There was something terribly uncanny in this old woman, a curious, insinuating, fascinating power.

As he yielded his hand to her he closely scanned her face, and saw that, scarred as it was by the wind and storm of many years, there were traces of the splendid beauty of her maidenhood.

As we see in the fragments of a glorious ruin evidence of a past magnificence, so did he see in that wild, eager face indications of the charms she had once possessed.

"See here," she said, tracing the lines upon his hand, "you came here to hide from the world; but it cannot be. Duty, the force of circumstances, and other things will drag you from here. You are doomed to wander about the earth for many days.

"Not seeking aught for yourself," she went on, passionately, "but to save the ingrate from ruin. You love the brother who despises you—you offer him the hand of affection, and he gives you back the stare of coldness, indifference, and worse. Nay, more. When you have done all to save him—when you HAVE saved him—it shall be his hand that strikes you down and leaves you for the wolves to pick your bones."

"Enough!" cried Hal. "I'll hear no more of such idle stuff. Here is money for you. Let it end."

"Keep your money for yourself," she cried; "you

will need it, and ere the sun goes down to-night you will know that I have told you nothing but the truth. They call me witch, but I am no witch, save that I know some things which others think are hidden from me."

"Why should you take an interest in me?" asked Hal, struggling with the emotion the strange interview had called into play.

"Ah! why?" she wailed. "If I told you, you would mock me."

"No, indeed!"

"Well, you would give me some courtly phrases, and laugh in your sleeve. What else could you do? For what sympathy could this tattered form of mine expect from one in the pride of his youth and beauty?"

"You do not know me so well as you profess to do," he answered, "or you would not speak in that way."

"They were words wrung from a riven heart," she said. "Do you not despise me?"

"No," he said.

"I believe you, oh! Hal o' the Heath," she said. "Well, you must go far from here. We may never meet again; I cannot tell. Will you take a blessing from me?"

There was a weird grace in her movements as she raised her arms, and he, governed by a feeling he could not resist, slowly sank upon one knee, and bent his head.

"In all your coming days, through all the perils of the time to come, may Heaven—who has given solace even to my broken heart, and helped me to bear the eternity of solitude I have known—be your guide and support! May the bold, brave, honest spirit now in your heart be ever with you, and the end of your wanderings be peace!"

He had taken off his cap, and as she finished her benediction she stooped and touched his crisp, close hair with her lips.

Then, with a swift step, widely different from her usual broken gait, she glided away.

CHAPTER II.

THE REVELRY IN THE OLD HALL—ARRIVAL OF A
STRANGER IN DISTRESS — WHO ROBBED THE
BANKER?

AT the time of our story there stood, about thirteen miles
on the south side of London, a fine old house known as
Spendeigh Hall.

For more than two centuries it had been owned and
occupied by the Warrington family, once people of great
importance in the county, but at the time we speak of
fallen into decay.

For this they had only to thank themselves.

The last three generations had been very wild. Money
was spent like water, the estate mortgaged, and when
Louis, one of the last of the race, came into possession of
his property there was little left for him to spend.

But somehow he had kept up the family hospitality for
two years, and now we find the old park, one dark
November night, ablaze with light, and guests assembled
in the vast dining-room.

They were all men, and mostly young—the "bloods"
and "bucks" of the neighbourhood—the ne'er-do-wells of
many a noble family.

But there was one member of the party who was missing,
and that was the host.

He had ridden out early that afternoon and had not
returned.

So said Terrant, his valet and factotum, a young man
with a sharp face and quiet ways, supposed to be deep in
the confidence of his master.

The absence of the host at the time when dinner ought
to be served must be a serious matter in most cases ; but
it was not so in this instance.

Louis Warrington's friends were accustomed to making
themselves at home in Spendeigh Hall, and as he was not
there they proceeded to kill time in the manner most
agreeable to them.

One group fell to story-telling and laughing over jests
afloat at the time; half-a-dozen began to gamble with

dice, and as many more with cards.

Only one did nothing but look on.

This was Jason Ferrell, a young man with an old face that was like a mask, so far as hiding whatever might be behind it.

He was the son of a successful lawyer and money-lender, who held the principal mortgage on the Warrington estate.

He professed to be as wild and reckless as the rest; but it was noted that he gambled very little, drank sparingly, and never shared in any wild freak likely to bring him into collision with the authorities.

He was a well-made fellow enough, and his face at a first glance might have been considered handsome; but a closer inspection showed that it was hard, unrelenting, cruel, and cunning.

There was a positively malevolent look on his face as he watched the young fellows disporting themselves.

He knew well enough which way they were going.

They were all fish for the parental net.

Some had been caught, and were hopelessly floundering therein.

Others were dallying outside the meshes, and the rest were pretty well sure to come in by-and-bye.

"Half-past seven," cried out a fair-haired youth named Guy Mainwaring, "and Louis not here. I vote we order dinner."

"Hear—hear!" cried a dozen voices.

"He's got some love business on," continued Guy, with a light laugh, "and he can't expect our appetites to wait for him. What ho! there."

He had opened the door and called aloud down the passage.

In response a grave, grey-headed servitor appeared.

"Dinner, my friend," said Guy; "let it be served."

"Pardon me, sir," was the reply, "but my master has not returned."

"It's your master's duty to be here," said Guy; "and, failing that duty, he will not blame hungry men for demanding something to eat."

"If you will take the responsibility," said the old man, "dinner shall be put on the table."

"That will I right willingly." replied Guy. "Hasten you, old man, lest we, for lack of something better, should pick your bones."

The table was already prepared, and only the joints remained to be put thereon.

Half-a-dozen men speedily performed this office, guided by the grey-headed servitor.

"Who takes the head of the table?" cried Guy.

Again the grey-headed servitor spoke.

"I beseech you, gentlemen, not to usurp that place. My master may yet appear."

"Nonsense!" said Guy. "We can't sit down without some sort of host. I vote that Jason Ferrell takes the chair. He will soon have a right to it—and many others, if I am not mistaken."

Jason hung back, but the thoughtless young fellows would take no refusal from him, and he was literally forced into the seat.

"Let us see how you can play the host," said David Theselton, a pale-faced, dissipated man of five or six and twenty. "Come, smile and look gracious. Order the wine bottle to be passed quickly. Begin the feast by giving us a toast."

"Really," returned Jason Ferrell, "I would rather not."

"But you must," chorussed half-a-score voices.

"I haven't got a toast to give," he urged.

"Nay, then, I will find you one," cried Guy Main-waring. "Fill your glasses, gentlemen, and stand up."

The glasses were soon charged, and the whole body of madcaps rose to their feet.

Jason Ferrell rose also, with a sickly smile on his face. He did not quite see the humour of the thing.

"Now the toast," said Guy. "Repeat it after me, you neat and trim limb of the law—'Confusion to all legal knaves and robbers!'"

"That's an insult!" said Jason.

"If you object to it you have your remedy," remarked

Guy, significantly.

Jason Ferrell bit his lip and raised his glass.

At that moment a tall, graceful young fellow glided up behind him and laid hold of the glass he held.

"I will drink the toast for you," he said, and with his disengaged hand he jerked Jason Ferrell from the chair.

"Louis! It's Louis! Hurrah!" cried the others.

"Yes, gentlemen," said the young host; "here I am with many apologies for my absence; but I have had important business to attend to. The toast, gentlemen— 'Confusion to all LEGAL knaves and robbers!'"

"Jason Ferrell ought to drink it," urged Guy, as the empty glasses were set down.

"Jason Ferrell drinks no m re in my house," said Louis, with flashing eyes. "His worthy father promised yesterday to renew the mortgage on Spendeigh; this afternoon he sends me notice that it is his intention to close at once."

"I am not accountable for what my father does," said Jason, sulkily.

"Granted. But, knowing what you know—"

"I know nothing."

"Don't lie, you strip of parchment, for I now know that you, while shamming to be one of us, have only been playing the part of spy for your father. You see the door."

"You will be sorry for this before long," said Jason Ferrell. "My father and I are not good friends."

"By my faith! must I speak twice?" cried Louis, leaping to his feet. "The door! Begone! or I will clip your ears for you."

Jason waited no longer, but retired with all speed. He stopped just one moment at the door to look back upon the party with angry eyes, and then disappeared.

"Gentlemen," said Louis, "we may now eat our dinner with some relish. I have long suspected that fellow playing *bon vivant* with us to be shamming. The beggar was seen at the Warrington Arms this morning with two bailiffs positively laden with writs. He spent an hour there arranging a campaign by which many of us will suffer."

"Why did you not keep him here," asked Guy, "and give him a dinner of parchment? I would have crammed the first course down his throat."

"Let him go," said Louis, "and for to-night be forgotten. Gentlemen, this is my last night in my old home. Let it be one worthy to call a leave-taking."

A chorus of sympathetic cries and denouncement of the lawyer rose up from the table, but Louis called for silence.

"It would have come one day," he said; "why not now? To dinner, and remember, the more we eat and drink to-night the less for the wolves to-morrow."

No gayer throng ever sat at the table.

The wine kept time with the rapid changes of dishes, and the merry jest went round. Louis, if he had any care for his change of fortune, or anxiety concerning the future, showed no traces of it. He was the merriest of them all.

Behind his chair stood the old servitor, with bowed head. He had served in the family from boyhood, and the blow fell heavily upon him in his old age.

Spendeigh had been his home, and there was no other place in the wide world that ever could be home again to him.

In the midst of the mirth the sound of the bell at the outer gate reached the old man's ears. It was only rung by visitors and friends, and some person of importance must have pulled it to ring so loudly.

He bent over his master's chair, and spoke softly but clearly in his ear.

"Master, there is somebody at the gate. Whom do you expect?"

"Why, nobody, old Marbury," replied Louis; "but whoever it is bring him in, unless it be a lawyer or bailiff. If it is either of these gentry, give him a crust of bread and a mug of beer and bid him pass on. We must e'en be hospitable to all to-night."

The old man sighed deeply and walked slowly from the room. From thence a passage led to the hall, and quickening his footsteps on hearing loud voices, he soon came in view of the unexpected arrival.

It was a tall, portly man, with a florid face, quietly dressed, and bearing in his person the marks of a high respectability.

He was gesticulating violently, and abusing two footmen who were barring his way.

"I tell you," he said, "that I must and will come in. What matters if I am a stranger? I have been robbed, my servants have fled, and the horses broke from my carriage. I will not be denied!"

"Stand aside," said the old servitor to the underlings, "and let the gentleman come in. You say you have been robbed?"

"Yes, and of a heavy sum," was the answer. "Ten thousand pounds in notes and gold. It was a planned thing—I swear it!"

"You travel with a large sum," said Marbury, gravely.

"It is not so large to me as it is to some people," replied the stranger, proudly. "I am Abraham Crome, the banker."

Marbury bowed to the man, who bore a name associated at the time with great wealth and unbounded credit.

"Come in, sir," he said; "my master will give you shelter for the night, and such poor fare as he has at his command. May I ask, sir, if you can give a description of the thieves?"

"Thieves!" cried the banker, hotly; "there were not thieves, only a thief—*One*! A man, single-handed, scared my knaves, cut the traces of my horses, and robbed me!"

"Possibly one of the notorious thieves who are known to infest these parts," suggested Marbury. "You saw his face?"

"I saw a mask the villain wore—no more," said the banker; "but give me something to drink. I've been blundering here and there, into ditches, up against posts and brambles and trees in the darkness, until I saw the lights of this house and crawled hither. I am half dead!"

"You shall have some wine," Marbury said, "and make such change in your attire as is possible. Then my master will be glad to see you at the table."

"And right glad shall I be to join him," said the banker. "Ten thousand pounds taken by one man, and he a whipper-snapper that one of my big, lumbering curs of servants ought to have swallowed. But I will bring the brute to the gallows, if it costs me half my fortune."

Dinner was more than half over when the banker was ushered into the room.

The portly man of high respectability, and ordinarily of great gravity of demeanour, was evidently taken aback on seeing such a riotous company. Louis Warrington had already been apprised of his coming, and a seat had been prepared for the stranger on his right hand.

"Are there no ladies in the house?" the banker asked.

"My master is not married," replied Marbury.

"Humph," muttered the banker; "I have fallen on a nest of young hawks, but it is too late to go back, and I cannot give up my dinner."

As he approached the table Louis, marking his coming reflected in a pier-glass opposite, rose to his feet and turned to greet him.

The action was observed, and the roars of noisy talk instantly subsided.

"Welcome, sir," said Louis, "to such poor fare as we can give you, and excuse the lack of congenial company."

"I have nothing to excuse," replied the banker, courteously, "and your fare will be as welcome to me as ever was food to hungry man."

He took the proffered hand, and they sat down.

Louis filled up a glass with wine and pledged him.

Marbury put food before the guest.

"I understand, sir, from my servant," said Louis, "that you have been robbed?"

"Ay! that I have," replied Abraham Crome; "but I'll be even with the villain. He shall be punished, if money and good officers can bring him to the gallows."

"You will make sure first that he deserves hanging?"

"Deserve it?" cried the banker; "of course he does."

"But there are robbers and robbers."

"What do you mean?"

" Why, some rob from choice, others from necessity. One man takes money, intending to return it—"

" He is a thief still," said the banker, " and deserves hanging."

" But suppose he did it under the influence of a moment of frenzy ?" replied Louis.

" I would hang him still," said the banker.

" Or, let us suppose, that having done it he repents and desired to return that which he had taken ?"

" I would not forgive him.   He should hang—hang, I say."   And the infuriated banker glared savagely about him in search of a responsive look in the eyes of others.

But he got none.   Whatever they might have thought of the robber, they had no sympathy with this unforgiving man.

" The money is nothing to me—nothing, I say," he went on, bombastically; " but the fellow has dared to stop me— Abraham Crome, the banker—financial agent to kings at home and abroad—one of the bulwarks of the nation."

Louis looked at him very quietly, and filled his glass again.

" Drink," he said, deliberately, " to the speedy capture of that robber.   Comrades all ! drink to the speedy revenge of Abraham Crome, the banker.

As he spoke the bell of the outer door clanged, and Louis started from his chair.

" What now !" he cried.   " Is there yet another stranger to come here to-night ?"

His face was pale, and he shivered as one overcome by terror, and as the door opened a cry burst from his lips.

" Hal," he said, with a fierce gesture, " you here? Did I not forbid you to darken these doors again ?"

" For all that," said Hal, " I am here, Louis, and I would speak to you alone."

"Hal o' the Heath! A word with you!" she cried.

CHAPTER III.
THE TWO BROTHERS—THE END OF THE ORGIE.

THE two brothers stood face to face.

They were very much alike in face and figure, but the expression and the bearing was different.

Louis looked like what he was—a careless, reckless, fallen man, while Hal had the upright, fearless courage and noble expression of true nobility.

The old banker looked from one to the other with a critical eye, wondering why they should be so alike and yet so unlike. He was not a very keen judge of human nature.

"Louis," said Hal, "I must speak to you alone."

"Why?" cried Louis. "There are no secrets between us."

"There were none once," said Hal, sadly; "but what I have to say to you cannot be uttered in the presence of a stranger."

"Is it a secret confession?"

"If you would have it so—yes."

Louis turned to the banker, and bowing to him in mock politeness, said—

"You will forgive me, I hope, leaving you for awhile alone?"

"Oh! don't apologise," said the banker; "but you will excuse me if I say that I don't quite—well, understand you."

"We will excuse anything," said Louis, with a sneer. "Now, Hal, I am at your service."

He opened a door on the left side of the room, and the two brothers passed into a small apartment, fitted up and used as a waiting-room.

"Now, Hal, what have you to say?—tell me quickly," said Louis, "for I am in no mood for the old sing-song."

"The old sing-song," said Hal, "was a sad song. We brothers have been brothers only in name for many years."

"Different habits, dear boy."

"Yes; but it was not that alone why I left you. It is

true that I am ashamed of the dishonour, and—"

"Stop, Hal! I won't hear a word of that—it's the old, old cant."

"Cant or not, it has come to this—that you, in idleness and extravagrance, have robbed me of my only retreat."

"Robbed you? By my faith," said Louis, "it is all in the family estate, and it is, or rather was, MINE."

"By the miserable law of primogeniture," said Hal, bitterly; "but have you forgotten our mother's dying injunction? The house on the heath and the small rental attached to it she asked you to give me. You gave it to me by word—by deed you have taken it back again."

"It had to go," said Louis. "I was devilishly hard up."

"Ferrell came to me," said Hal, "with the tidings that it was no longer my home. He offered me the use of it FOR A WEEK, a charitable offer to the fallen. I left it at once and came hither. Would that I had remained."

"Well, it was foolish to refuse so good an offer," said Louis.

"Not for myself," said Hal, "and yet for myself as well as you. Louis, what have you done to-night?"

"Done to-night?" said Louis, cautiously. "Let me see. I have been over to the inn, and—"

"Oh! brother mine," said Hal, "repair the wrong you have done. Give him back his money. Say it was a jest. Perhaps it *was* a jest."

"His money!" said Louis, wonderingly. "What do you mean?"

"You robbed a man to-night," said Hal. "I did not see you do it, but I was coming hither and heard his cries for help. I went to his aid and saw you riding away. You cast this mask into the bushes." Hal drew a crape mask from his pocket. "I picked it up, wondering what it all meant. Then came the man tearing by, so wild with terror that he did not notice me. I saw it all then, Louis. You, the elder, the head of the house of Warrington, ROBBED him!"

"Yes, I did," said Louis, with a yawn, "but I will repay him some day."

"Repay him now."

"I have a scheme of going ahead to make money, but it required money to start with. Ferrell would lend me no more, and to attempt to work for it would be absurd, so I borrowed of an unwilling stranger."

"Oh! Louis, this is pitiful and terrible."

"Hark you, Hal!" said Louis, with sudden ferocity. He cast aside his suave demeanour as if it were a garment. "You were a sneak always."

"Louis!"

"A sneak and a cur. Go now and betray me. Hand me over to this man, who will make a felon of me."

"Louis," said Hal, "loving you as I do I cannot betray you."

"I will not trust you," said Louis. "Hark you! This place is not your home or mine from henceforth. You go your way and I will go mine."

"Give back the money to the man!"

"In my own good time," said Louis, "and not yours. Will you go?"

"He shall have his money."

Louis walked to the mantel-piece and put a hand upon the bell rope.

"I will give you," he said, "two minutes to be gone. If you stay beyond that time I will give *you* into custody for highway robbery."

"Give *me* into custody?" said Hal.

"Yes. What are you doing here?" asked Louis— "penniless, with a crape mask in your pocket, and your agitated bearing? Ask any man of the world who looks most like the thief now—you or I?"

"Louis," said Hal, "you were ever of a daring, evil spirit, and I know you would do this thing if I drove you to it. I will not do so for the love I bear you; in spite of all that I have suffered at your hands, I yield, with the hope that one day you may repent and your heart soften towards me, or that you may, for the honour of our name, amend your ways."

"Your time has almost expired." said Louis, looking at his watch.

"I am going," replied Hal. "One last word. Farewell Henceforth I am a stranger to the land of my birth. Farewell to home and you! In some far-off land I will seek to live unheard of and forgotten. One thing will cheer me, my name and honour is unstained. What grief I may feel will be for the brother I loved; the brother who had a heart of stone. Farewell!"

He walked from the room erect, and so they parted, —the two brothers in name and blood—to meet no more in the land that gave them birth.

Louis remained for a few seconds with his arm resting on the mantel-piece, his face impassive, and his eyes on the door, as if he expected Hal to return.

But the only sounds he heard were the voices of the banker and his friends, the latter talking in an unwonted subdued tone.

The calm upon them was an unnatural one.

It was as if they were holding their breath in expectation of some great catastrophe.

"He will keep his word and go away," said Louis, with a sigh of relief. "So far I am safe."

Then he sauntered back into the other room, and said, with a smile—

"The good man has come and gone and we can resume our merry evening. Now, Crome, we will cheer you up as well as we can to console you for your loss."

"I am usually spoken of as MISTER Abraham Crome," said the banker, haughtily.

"We have no misters here," replied Louis, "being all good fellows. For one night you may lay aside your city dignity. I am Louis Warrington.

"I have heard of you," said the banker, with a frown, "from my lawyer, Mr. Ferrell."

"Who, of course, told you all sorts of good things about me?" said Louis, grimly.

"No, young sir, he has not," said the banker. "I regret to say that his opinion of you and your companions —these gentlemen here—is not exactly favourable."

"Talk of robbers," cried Louis, with a sudden burst of passion, "there is one? That knave ought to have been hanged years ago."

"Sir," said the banker, "I consider Mr. Ferrell to be my friend."

"I beg your pardon," said Louis. "I spoke in haste. Then to-night Mr. Ferrell shall be all you think he is. Gentlemen, the health of our gracious guest, Mr. Abraham Crome, and his friend, Lawyer Ferrell, all standing—no heel-taps."

The banker had a shrewd suspicion that he was the victim of sarcasm; but the toast was drunk with much noise and clamour, which passed for enthusiasm.

Old Marbury looked gravely on, his eyes resting frequently with a strange look of interest on his master's face.

The banker ate and drank a great deal before he had satisfied his wants.

He evidently belonged to that class of good feeders who eat about five times their share of the good things of this earth.

The subject of the robbery was not renewed at the table.

After the cloth was cleared cards and dice were again introduced.

The banker looked on with an air of haughty superiority to their vices, and Louis did not, as usual, play.

He sat looking on with a growing moodiness until the banker, by sundry mighty yawns, indicated that he was ready for bed.

Louis rose up and begged to be allowed to escort him to his room.

Marbury was ready with four strong men, each bearing a wax candle, to do honour to their guest.

With two candles before and two behind, the party ascended the stairs, Marbury going on well in front to open the chamber door.

Louis entered the room with his guest and saw that all was comfortable—a couch with ample covering, and a fire burning on the hearth.

"One word, sir," said Louis, as he stood by the fire after Marbury and the servants had gone. "You adhere to your statement—that you will not forgive the offender?"

"I do," replied the banker. "I will never forgive a man who robs me."

"It is enough," said Louis, "and I will say no more—beneath my roof. At another time, and in a more fitting place, I may renew the subject."

Deep bows were exchanged, and they parted for the night.

Louis strode into the corridor, and crossing to the other side opened the door of another room.

This was the place where he kept his papers, books, swords, pistols, and all the nick-nacks of a bachelor's life.

Old Marbury was there walking slowly to and fro.

He stopped when he saw his young master, and turned on him a face most piteous in its expression.

"What ails you, old Faithful?" said Louis.

"Master," said Marbury, holding out his hands, clasped together, "what have you done?"

"That which cannot be recalled," said Louis. "We cannot all be good men. There is light and shade all over the world. If you like to have it so, I am the shade and Hal is the light of the house of Warrington."

"Heaven help you both!" groaned the old man, as he walked from the room with clasped hands.

The story of the crime committed by Louis, a deed of madness, can be briefly told. It is simply a replica of a deed of one of the cowardly highwaymen of a century ago.

On the bare chance of getting *something* to assist him in his wild schemes he went out to rob; and chance led him across the banker's path.

He rode up to the carriage and called on the coachman to stop.

This worthy and the footman beside him tumbled off their seats and fled.

The horses plunged about, overturning the coach, and Louis cut the traces. Set free they galloped away.

As for the banker, he had not the heart of a mouse, and

on his knees begged for mercy.

"Give me your money—money only," said Louis.

And with a palsied hand Abraham Crome handed to him a box containing the notes.

It was done—there was no recall—and Louis, in a frenzy of excitement, rode away with his prize.

Before he reached home he was cool again, but he wished he had not done the deed.

Vague thoughts of restitution uprose before him, but there was poverty at the door, and he clung to what he had gained.

The banker's expressed resolution to show no mercy also hardened him, and Hal's coming had made him dogged. He would not go back.

"What is an outlaw?" he asked himself. "What does the world say of Robin Hood now? He took from the rich to give to the poor. Bah! I hate the sickly sentimentality of that saying. I'll take from the rich because I want it. It is done. I have crossed the stream, and to-day I burn my boats behind me. The head of the Warringtons is an outlaw."

Then he rang the bell, and bade a servant send his valet to him.

Terrant came quietly into the room, and stood near the table waiting to be addressed.

Louis traversed the room two or three times more before speaking.

"I sent for you," he said, at last, "because you are the one man about me able and willing to do what I want done to-night."

"I am ready, sir," replied Terrant, quietly.

"You must ride to Portsmouth with all speed, and take a letter I will write to James Medley.

"Where shall I find him, sir?"

"At the Blue Posts Inn," Louis said, as he sat down and began to write.

The letter was very brief, and having folded and sealed it he gave it to his follower.

"Terrant," he said, "have you any ties here?"

"None at all, sir," the man replied.

"Then you would turn your back upon the place without much grief?"

"I can't say that, sir, but if YOU are going—"

"Terrant," said Louis, "it is all over here. It would be childish to conceal the truth or cry over it. I have to go to-morrow, and I shall never return. You will await my coming at Portsmouth."

"Master Louis," said Terrant, bending over the table and looking straight into his face, "I know what you have done to-night. Don't stop here another hour. Let us ride away together. I've got a reason for it."

"No," replied Louis, "not until to-morrow. I have a guest in the house, and the laws of hospitality must be observed. Besides I have one to see before I go."

"Ah! master," said Terrant, sadly, "it's the old story. It's a HER, and I can't see why you want to see her now. Sir Charles don't look upon your suit now with any favour, but now—"

"I understand you, Terrant" interposed Louis, "but for all I shall do as I have arranged. Away with you now. Here is money, get good horses when you change, and lose not a moment."

Terrant took the purse tended him, bowed, and left the room without another word.

Louis shortly after followed, and rejoined his boisterous friends below.

Barely had he left the room when a heavy curtain drawn across the window begun to vibrate, and presently the face of Jason Ferrell slowly appeared in the folds.

It was pale with excitement, and his eyes shone with ferocious triumph.

He had made a great discovery that placed Louis Warrington, whom he hated, absolutely in his power.

He hated Louis for many reasons, most potent of all that he stood between the lawyer's son and the lovely Lucy Danebury.

Sir Charles was a needy baronet, one of the many birds snared by the lawyer Ferrell, and he would have put no bar against Jason in his wooing, averse as he instinctively was to such a *liaison*.

But when the nameless one drives, men needs must go whither he takes them.

Jason, having turned out of the dining-room, finding no servants about, and not fearing immediate interruption, sneaked up to Louis' room to see if he could find any letter for Lucy lying about.

He wanted to know the exact relations between them, and to find out some joint in the armour of their love between which he could insert some poisoned dart.

But, having once got into the room, it was not easy to get out again.

Thrice he essayed to do so, but somebody moving in the corridor drove him back again, and so it happened that he, without any danger on his part, was made acquainted with facts that gave him the power of ruining Louis utterly.

His task now was to get away and return with all speed with officers of the law, and boldly arrest and charge Louis with his crime.

Everything favoured him. He got out of the house without being observed, and the stables were unlocked, with a lighted lantern suspended from the roof.

The horse he rode thither on was lying down, well fed and rested. The saddle was handy, and in five minutes he was riding with all speed to the nearest station.

Meanwhile, Louis had found his guests pretty well played out. They had drunk and gambled for awhile, and then from flagging in the absence of their host, they were talking of going homeward.

Louis made no attempt to infuse new life into the evening, and the party broke up. Sleepy servitors, dozing before the kitchen fire, were roused and bidden to bring the horses round to the door.

Then came the final parting with all his old friends.

Glasses were filled to the brim, and they all stood up with more or less steadiness.

"Gentlemen," said Louis, "this is our parting glass. No vain regrets—no sympathy, please. When a man has had his fling, it is folly to whine over what follows. A health to you, one and all."

They drank to his with wild cries and cheers that were heard far away from the hall. The glasses they drank from were dashed to the ground to prevent their being used for a less worthy toast. Hands met, and a few parting words were spoken.

It was dark without, but the band of madcaps cared nothing for that. One by one they leaped into the saddle and rode away as if it had been high noonday.

Louis went gloomily enough to bed. Now that he was alone, and the bubbling excitement of the evening dying down, he was beginning to realise his true position.

But he was not sorry for the crime he had committed, nor softened towards Hal. He only feared being found out, and he hated his brother yet the more.

To bed he went, to fall into a fitful sleep and be aroused in the middle of the night by being dragged from his bed.

The officers of justice were upon him. He fought for liberty, but they overmastered him, and in the murky darkness he was taken away from the home of his forefathers, never to look upon it again.

* * * * * * * * *

Oh! brief be this part of his miserable story. He was tried, convicted, and sentenced to fifteen years' penal servitude ; and in the dismal cell of his self-earned prison we must leave him for the time.

CHAPTER IV.

IN A FAR-OFF LAND—THE TWO WANDERERS—A WARNING—ACROSS A FRAIL BRIDGE.

IT was high noon, and a scorching sun glared down from a cloudless sky upon two travellers wandering through a scene of great natural beauty.

The land was a mixture of mountain and vale. Rich flowers abounded, and from the sides of a vast mountain, which towered up to the clouds, poured a broad cascade.

From rock to rock it dashed and leaped in its haste to get into the sweet plains. In some places it assumed the proportions of a fall—the water taking a leap sheer down a hundred feet or more.

This wild watercourse lay in the travellers' path, and

they were seeking a way across it.

To go higher was a task that would have taxed the energies of many a hardy mountaineer ; to go lower might lead them to a river without a ford, and these men had neither a boat nor the means to build one.

Halting, they stood upon a rock, gazing downward.

At their feet ran the turbid water-course, a glorious spectacle !

"It's pretty, Master Hal ; but it be mighty inconvenient just now."

"So it is, Grip, for we must get out of this horrible country. We may have stout hearts, but we have not the strength to beat a whole tribe."

Thus did Grip and Hal comment upon the situation.

Not with any display of fear, but in the cooler way of men who have travelled and acquired the traveller's nerve.

For a whole year they had been going here and there, to find themselves at last in what the natives called in their vernacular the Land of Jewels.

Of these people we shall see a little more anon. Hal and Grip had seen enough of them already.

"Once across this cascade," said Hal, "and we shall come to the Land of Rest, among a peaceful people."

"Heaven send us there quickly, Master Hal," replied Grip, "for, if I mistake not, the people here are cannibals, and I have no taste for being toasted, even to make a breakfast for so big a man as Peruquio, the King of the Land of Jewels."

"Well said, Grip," replied Hal. "Just my sentiments exactly. But tell me, old friend, how it is to be done ?"

"Whoop—ta—whoo—a !"

A cry broke upon them, and both turned quickly to see who it was that had thus disturbed them.

Bounding from rock to rock towards them came a swarthy savage with spear and shield.

His body was decorated with fantastically-mounted jewels.

In his coarse, black hair feathers were fastened, and as he bounded along they fluttered in the wind, giving to his movements the appearance of even greater activity than really existed.

"Whoop—ta—whoo—a !"

It was a piercing, unearthly, savage cry that rung in the ears of the travellers with anything but a musical sound.

But they did not budge.

Each had a rifle which they could have used and brought down the savage like a partridge; but they forbore, and waited until he was quite near.

He dashed up to within a few feet of them, and then pulled up as suddenly as a sharply-reined restive horse.

"You are not gone?" he said, in a deep-toned gutteral way, speaking in his own tongue.

Hal had picked up a little of it during a brief but unpleasant sojourn among these people.

"No," he said.

"The king commanded," said the savage.   "Why still here?"

"Because we have not found the road," said Hal. "We go one way—to find the earth split for miles in an impassable gulf—we try the other, and see that we have a huge watercourse to bar our way."

"I sha'n't go," said the savage, grimly; "but you must go."

There was just a faint indication of humour in his wild face that led Hal to think that he and Grip were the victims of a huge practical joke.

The way they entered the land was guarded by the king and his tribe—other way out there was none.

"You must go," the savage said, ignoring the words of Hal.

"Show us the way?" said Hal.

The savage pointed up the mountain, and signified by a motion of his arm that there the cascade was spanned by a bridge.

"No other way," he said.   "Go—or when sun gone, you die."

With another fierce cry he threw up his arms and bounded away.

They saw him leap from rock to rock, as agile as a goat, and finally disappear in a belt of wood.

Master and man looked at each other.

"Grip!"

"Master Hal."

"What do you think of the bridge?"

Grip looked doubtful.

"It seems to me, master, they are sending us here and there - toying with us, playing with us cat and mouse fashion—knowing that we cannot get away."

"When worst comes to worst," said Hal, "I will sell my life dearly. Not that I think so much of it on my own account, but on yours, Grip."

"What's mine is yours, master, and I do not value my life."

"For all that," said Hal, sadly, "I have no right to take it. Say, old friend, shall we try the mountain side?"

"As well one way as the other, master. For my own part I think there is no way out of this."

"Come, then, we have from now till sun down, and then the end, if it must be so."

So they began the ascent—as arduous as that of climbing a torn and rugged pyramid.

Here and there narrow rents of unknown depth barred the way, and across them they fearlessly leaped.

Stones, dislodged by their feet, dashed down these openings rattling and booming in the secret bowels of the mountains.

Between the rocks were patches that were like gardens, for there the earth was rich, and orchids and other flowers rare enough in our home country, grew in great profusion.

And now the cascade, after a hour's toil, takes a turn to the right, and opens up another seemingly endless pile of mountains, and far over head they espy the bridge.

It was only the trunk of a huge tree that had either fallen or been thrown across a point in the watercourse where the rocks rose up and leant inward like tottering walls.

Above and below was the cascade roaring, leaping, dashing, swirling on its turbid way.

"Master Hal," said Grip, "we can never cross that.'

"We can try," said Hal, cheerily.

So on they went, and nearly another hour elapsed ere they reached the one frail road to lead them from savage land to life and liberty.

It was reached, and they lay down to rest by the gnarled roots.

Both were wearied, but Nature was kind to them.

Under the lee of a big rock in a bed of soft, rich earth some wild grapes were ripening in the sun.

Grip gathered a few, and to the weary travellers they were even food and drink.

"Now, Grip," said Hal, rising, "we must make the venture while there is full light in the sky."

"Master Hal," said Grip, "no man could ever keep a footing there."

"Come, Grip! you used to be so stout of heart."

"And I am stout of heart now, Master Hal. But you —you—"

"Come, Grip! I will lead the way. Hold your rifle firmly, and use it to keep your balance."

He stepped boldly on to the fearful bridge; above him the leaping cascade, below a wilderness of rock and water.

Grip was pale, but it was true that he was not thinking of himself but of his young master.

Had he thought less of him and more of himself the catastrophe that took place might have been spared them.

Hal had proceeded about a dozen steps on his way, taking each step slowly and carefully when Grip, who was two paces in the rear, slipped and fell upon his leader.

In a moment Hal was thrown from the bridge, but Grip, who had fallen full length upon it, grasped his arm, and held him with the tenacity of despair.

"Steady, old friend!" cried Hal. "Don't lose your head or we must both go."

"Oh! Master Hal," moaned Grip.

He was holding on to the bridge with a tremendous grip of the knees and feet.

"How long can you hold, Grip?" asked Hal.

"Till my arms are torn off or my knees give way," gasped Grip.

"Steady!" said Hal. "Now, your other hand—there, hand to hand, old friend, as we should be in such a dread hour."

"Can't you climb up, Master Hal?" moaned Grip.

"No; I am not an acrobat," replied Hal. "I must drop. See! there are our rifles below on that rock. Now, if you can only get me there."

"Master Hal, you'd not have a whole bone in your body left."

"It is the only thing to do, Grip. If both go, we both must be lost. Men have fallen from great heights and not suffered much harm. Swing me gently to and fro, and when I give the word, let go."

"Oh! Master Hal, must it be?"

"Even so, Grip. Farewell, old friend, if I go to my death. We have no time to say more. You cannot hold on long now—one—two—let go!"

With a groan Grip let go, and wildly clutched the trunk of the tree in his arms as Hal fell like a plummet to the rocks on the border of the cascade below.

CHAPTER V.

NOT DEAD—A DAY IN HIDING—DOWN THE RAPIDS.

GRIP clung to the tree to save himself from falling. All things swam before him, and the roar of the waters seemed to have multiplied tenfold in his ears.

To him the pain he felt was more terrible than anything he had hitherto known—it was more than bodily pain, it was the extreme agony of the spirit.

He could not trust himself to look down, but backed inch by inch until he found himself once more on terra firma.

Then he slowly raised himself up and looked below.

On a rock lay Hal, stretched out as he had fallen, with the stillness of death upon him.

But was it death?

Grip was no sentimentalist, a believer in dreams, but at all times a man of action.

Breathing in a broken way a prayer for the safety of his young master, he leaped down from rock to rock to go to his aid.

And not a moment too soon.

For now, as if sprung from the ethereal blue, some vultures, those sharks of the air, were bearing down upon the fallen form, ready to rend and devour it even if life were not wholly extinct.

Grip shouted, or tried to shout, but his voice was feeble, and the roar of the waters drowned it.

Even as he reached the prostrate form of his master the first vulture was upon him.

Its villainous head was raised to strike, and in another moment its talons would have been buried in that handsome face, but the maddened Grip struck at it with his bare fist, and dashed the bird of prey aside.

The blow told so far, but it neither killed nor stunned the vulture.

With a hoarse cry it righted itself, and with its brethren rose heavily in the air, and there circled round, disappointed, but still hopeful of prey.

Grip knelt beside Hal, and found he still breathed. Then he raised his limbs slowly and tenderly one by one, and found them safe and sound.

The great question of internal injuries now remained.

Grip's next care was to restore Hal to consciousness, and having filled his hat from a pool, formed in a hollow rock by the unceasing spray, he sprinkled his forehead.

Hal opened his eyes and gazed heavily around him, until he saw Grip, at whom he looked at in a wondering way.

"Master Hal, speak to me!" Grip cried.

"What has happened?" asked Hal.

"Oh! master—master," said Grip, "let me raise you a little. See. Don't that hurt you?"

"I feel," said Hal, "as if I had been sorely beaten."

Then he raised his eyes, and, seeing the tree-bridge above, a complete knowledge of recent events came back to him.

"Have I fallen so far and LIVE?" he asked.

"Master Hal, you have," said Grip. "It was Heaven's mercy. You must have touched yon ledge, with its bank of earth, first—look how crushed the flowers are—and have fallen from there to here. I could not—dare not—look when by your command I let go."

"Give me a hand," said Hal, "I think I can rise."

He got up with some difficulty, and stood upright with his knees shaking.

"It was a horrible fall," he said; "but all I feel of it is as if I were tired—worn out—and want a rest."

"We must find some place to hide for the night," said Grip, "and then to-morrow, if you can move, retrace our steps.'

"Perhaps we can travel at night," said Hal; "there is a moon."

The place in which they stood was a very secluded spot, owing to the cliff-like rocks that rose above their heads. It was a hollow, in fact, filled with huge pieces of rocks and trees tumbled one upon another by the action of water and tempest.

There were a score of hiding-places to screen them from ordinary observation, and Hal, with Grip's assistance, got safely into a small cave—one of Nature's chambers of the mountain.

There, on a dry sandy bed, Hal lay down, and Grip went in search of their rifles.

He was some time away, but as it was growing dark he came back with them. Both had happily fallen on the margin of the cascade, and, with the exception of a slight damage to the stock of Grip's, had suffered no injury.

The two men possessed between them about fifty rounds of ammunition, and thus had many lives of their foes at their mercy.

Hitherto they had forborne to use them on the natives, knowing that numbers must in the end prevail; but now, if attacked, they could and would sell their lives dearly.

Hal was not hungry or thirsty.

The feeling upon him was intense fatigue, and he soon

sank into a deep sleep.

It was a sleep of terrible fevered dreams at first. Much of the past came back to him, and he went through the scenes with his brother and old Marbury over and over again, until he suddenly found himself floating in still waters.

Then he dreamed no more.

When he awoke Grip was seated beside him, and a glad smile overspread the rugged face of the faithful fellow.

"Master Hal," he said, "how fare you now?"

"Well," replied Hal, "save that I am stiff and sore, as if I had been indulging in unwonted exercise, as, indeed, I have."

He added the latter words with a smile, a thing Grip had rarely of late seen upon his face.

After an effort he rose up and tried his limbs one by one.

They moved stiffly, but the fact of being able to move them at all was reassuring.

And now Grip had a surprise in store for him.

From behind a big stone he brought out some freshly-roasted meat, barely cold, and very appetising to a hungry man.

"Part of a mountain sheep, master," he said. "I shot it this morning by the first ray of light."

"It is more than welcome, Grip. But what of the sound of your rifle?"

"I do not think it could be heard far away with the noise of yon cataract. We must eat and be strong. I cut it up and roasted it with a fire I lighted in a cave a mile from here. The smoke could not be seen, for there was a morning mist upon the mountains."

"Good Grip!" was all Hal said.

With good meat for breakfast and water to drink they fared well for travellers in such a lonely region.

Hal felt stronger, but he was not in the trim for a resumption of their journey, and it was decided they should hide there all day, and at night return by the way they came, taking the course of the cataract, which, as Hal argued, must lead to a river, and from the river to the sea.

It was well that they decided to remain close that day, for the morning was yet young when Grip, peeping forth, saw a number of the natives overhead peering about the bridge.

One was pointing out to the others indications of the travellers having been upon it ; but none attempted to cross until a huge savage, all paint, feathers, and jewels—real jewels that glistened in the sunlight—appeared upon the scene.

From their hiding-place the two travellers watched his movements.

He appeared to be in a furious, disappointed mood, and Hal guessed, and guessed rightly, that the savages had been looking for their bodies below, and failing to find them had come up the mountain to see if the travellers had dared to traverse that perilous path.

Peruquio, the king, evidently believed they had crossed in safety, for he, in an authoritative way, bade some of his people attempt it also.

They all drew back.

He became imperative, and drawing his spear from its resting-place—a leather strap across his back—he fairly drove one wretched man upon the tree.

With faltering steps the doomed man made his way to the centre of the trunk, and then suddenly slipped and fell.

The travellers saw him turn twice in the air and dash down into the rushing water.

He was not killed by his fall.

They saw him borne downward, battling for his life, tossed from rock to rock like a toy, his eyes starting out of his head, his tongue lolling in the agonies of death, and finally disappear.

"Horrible !" said Hal, between his teeth.

Grip said nothing, but his set lips and colourless face spoke of the emotion the truly terrible scene inspired within him.

And now Peruquio ought to have been satisfied.

But, no !

Another of his subjects was commanded to make the

attempt, and met with a like fate.

Yet a third was ordered to offer himself up as a sacrifice for the palpable amusement it afforded the king.

Peruquio had evidently discovered a new source of royal fun.

The third man was equal to the emergency.

He RAN at the tree and skimmed across it like a bird, leaping on the opposite side with a shout that rose above the noise of waters.

All the savages applauded, and the king beckoned him back; but again this savage showed that he was not all fool.

He had had enough of Peruquio, and, bold in the sense of security from the king's wrath, he made a movement expressive of keen contempt for Peruquio, and dashed away out of sight.

No doubt it was a moment of supreme delight to him, as it was of mortification to his ruler.

Peruquio went on like a madman for some minutes, darting here and there with his spear, intending to avenge the insult he had received on the persons of the non-offenders.

The savages scattered right and left, dodging him with the agility of monkeys.

They popped out of sight and into sight again in such a ludicrous manner that both Hal and Grip laughed heartily but in a necessarily quiet way.

It was a pantomime of real life.

At last Peruquio became tired of his futile efforts to spear somebody, and stalked haughtily away.

His followers came out of their hiding-places and dis-appeared also.

"Gone," said Hal; "and I pray they may return no more to-day."

Return they did not, for, without a doubt, they believed the travellers had got safe away, and so spoilt one of Peruquio's jokes.

The day passed on and evening came, with a moon just entering its second quarter in the sky.

Hal declared he was strong enough to attempt to return,

and they set out on their perilous journey

Grip had made a package of a portion of the wild sheep he had cooked—enough, he reckoned, to last them two days—and strapped it on his shoulder wallet fashion.

Hal made no complaint, and to all Grip's whispered queries declared he was well as ever. They did not dare to speak aloud lest their voices should be conveyed to some watchful savage's ears.

All night long, with intervals of rest, they travelled, and, the way being downhill, recovered their lost ground, and descended to where the cascade reached a long reach of level water.

In the dim light it looked as it they had reached level ground, and, overjoyed, they lay down among some bushes and slept.

Grip was the first to wake, and when he opened his eyes the sun was high overhead, for it was about noon.

Before awaking Hal he stood up and cautiously looked about him.

He saw no sign of living being, but half-a-mile or so further on he beheld a dark object, shaped like a canoe, lying on the banks of the stream.

If it should prove to be a canoe here was a means of escape he had not hoped or looked for.

He aroused Hal and told him of the discovery he had made. Hal had younger eyes and keener sight, and he declared it *was* a canoe.

Nay, more, he could see the handle of a paddle sticking out of it.

"We must get to it, Grip," he said, "and waste no time, for perhaps the owner may appear and take it away."

"Breakfast first," said Grip. "We can eat and keep our eyes about us."

A hurried meal was partaken of, and then they started, keeping close under the shelter of the bushes that grew by the margin of the stream.

Unencumbered and unchecked they reached the canoe, and found it something beyond the ordinary workmanship of savages.

It was of cedar wood, gracefully shaped, and with seats

for two, and a pair of paddles, and covered at the ends.

The *inside* was ornamented with uncut, precious stones, and the handles of the paddles were similarly beautified.

Of the real nature and value of these our travellers knew nothing, nor was that the time to inspect them.

Boldly launching the canoe, they stepped in, Hal taking the forward seat.

"Do as I do, Grip," he said; "and sit steady. This is the style of boat that won't bear much rocking."

Hal knew how to use a paddle fairly well, and, having guided their boat into the middle of the rapid stream, they glided on their way.

The water was shallow, and flowed swiftly. At a racing pace they covered two or three miles, and then once more the thunder of falling waters fell upon their ears.

"Rapids ahead, Grip!" said Hal. "We must land and carry the canoe."

So intent had he been in guiding the canoe that he had scarce glanced towards the shore, but Grip had been watchful throughout.

He had seen dark moving specks in the distance which he thought might be savages in pursuit, but said not a word until he was pretty sure.

And then, as Hal spoke he drew his attention to the specks, which were growing larger.

"Master Hal," he said, "I think some of our old friends are not far away. There! to the right."

"It is so, Grip," said Hal. "We must keep on, and take our chance with the rapids. I have never attempted to shoot such places, but I have read how it is done. Sit still until the canoe goes to pieces, or turns over."

"I'll trust to you, Master Hal," said Grip, cheerily.

There was now no doubt they were being pursued.

The savages were coming on at a great rate, and their figure and style of dress, if dress it can be called, showed that they were indeed their old friends.

"We have got hold of the king's canoe," said Hal. "Perhaps that noble monarch usurped to himself the right of using the water."

It was more than likely it was so, for canoes would give his subjects the opportunity of crossing to the other shore, although landing, to Hal's eyes, seemed difficult, if not impossible.

Hal at first had some thoughts of attempting it, but he could see that there was a succession of shallows and deep pools of water which would debar them from getting there either in the canoe or on foot.

And the shore on the other side was a line of precipitous and apparently inaccessible cliffs.

Last, but not least, the canoe was now so near the rapids, and the stream ran so swiftly that any attempt to land, save on the southern side, would result in disaster.

An additional motive urged Hal to keep on.

He cared naught for money for money's sake, but he knew its value in dealing with the world, and he felt convinced that in the ornaments of the canoe he had the means of realising quite a little fortune.

Taking all things into consideration, his wisest and most hopeful course was to keep on.

The heads of the rapids were now in sight, and there the stream narrowed considerably.

The rush down must be tremendous.

Towards this point the savages were making.

It was a race between them and the canoe as to who should get there first.

If the canoe was the foremost it would go down the rapids with a velocity that would carry its passengers out of the reach of their foes.

If the savages got there first they would have a sure point of vantage, from which they could hurl their weapons at the two daring men.

The race was now very close.

Both bore down to the given point with a speed that promised they would meet there together.

It would be impossible for Hal and Grip to use their rifles, save for a chance shot, without taking sight, and that would be a mere waste of good ammunition.

On they came, canoe and men closing in on the head of the rapids.

"We shall arrive together, Grip," said Hal; "and all we can do is to sit still and let them make moving targets of us. But they cannot get more than one shot apiece at us."

"There are a hundred of them, Master Hal," said Grip, grimly.

There seemed to be fully that number, or more, and they were running racehorse pace.

And now the mouth of the rapids is reached, and the savages, yelling, are clambering up the rocks.

Spears are raised; the wild cries of the foemen mingle with the boom and screech of the waters.

Hal says nothing—he could not be heard if he did—but sits still and upright, ignoring the perils ashore, and with his eyes on the dangers ahead.

Whirr!

A spear whizzes by him, so close to his face it is like a flash of light before his eyes.

But he sits erect and stirs not an inch.

Another strikes the bow of the canoe and quivers there.

With a steady hand he steers the canoe clear of a rock, and goes down into what looks like a seething cauldron of bubbling waters and spray.

Another spear, and another—the air is thick with them; and Hal feels the canoe lurch a little, and a groan comes half-smothered to his ears.

Grip was wounded, and had fallen back in the canoe a dead weight and an additional peril.

"Strive as I may now," thought Hal, "I cannot save us."

And as the thought flashed through his mind the canoe swirled round in the foaming water, and then was dashed against a rock.

Hal found himself in the boiling water, fighting for his life.

But even then he had eyes for his faithful follower, whom he saw borne by, with the spear sticking in his breast, inanimate and a mere log upon the foaming rapids.

CHAPTER VI.

TWO SCENES—THE ESCAPE AND THE SHIPWRECK—A WONDERFUL MEETING.

WE must now call our readers' attention to two scenes which have an important bearing on our story. We will endeavour to describe them as briefly as possible.

The first deals with a cold autumn eve when three men were being carried in the direction of one of our great penal settlements in a train.

They had a compartment to themselves, for one of these men was in convict garb, and the others were two warders who had him in charge.

The prisoner, despite his hideous garb, looked like what he was—a handsome man.

It was wild Louis Warrington, who had served his nine months' preliminary punishment in Pentonville prison, and was now being borne away to the penal settlement at Dartmocr.

He was on good terms with the warders, who looked upon him as a *rara avis* in the way of prisoners.

His handsome face, his winning ways, had won upon them, and they were chatting together as if they were old friends.

"Oh! don't you fear," one of the warders said, "it isn't so very bad in penal servitude—is it, Jim?"

"No, Dave," replied the other warder.

"Work the oracle right," continued the first speaker, "and you will get allowances and liberties and lots of things."

"Some parties are so comfortable," said Jim, "that they are no sooner out than they want to get in again."

"You remember Ben the Bouncer?" said Dave.

"Rather," replied Jim.

"Wasn't he the life and soul of the Moor?"

"Yes; all that and more."

"Didn't he keep 'em all going looking after him? The way that man worked. Why, he was never without a letter or something from a pal outside, and he got his 'bacca as regular as the days came round; and if he had not tried to escape he might have gone on easy through the whole of his time."

"So he tried to escape?" said Louis, quickly.

"He did," chuckled Dave; "burrowed right under the prison, and got out; but it was a foggy night, and after wandering about and meeting with this sentry and that, he worked his way back right under the prison walls, and I'm blessed if he wasn't standing by the very gate looking about him when the fog lifted."

"Then he was seen, of course?" said Louis.

"Seen and shot down," said Dave, complacently. "He got a bullet in his thigh, and was laid up in the infirmary for five months."

"Prisoners do escape now and then?" said Louis, carelessly.

"Never from Dartmoor or Portland," replied Jim, "though many have tried it. There's too many circles of sentries, and the country is against it."

"Well, I am not going to try it," said Louis. "Ingenuity is not in my line. I was not born and bred to a convict life like some of them."

"You've dropped into it by a slip like many a one," said Jim; "and all you've got to do is to get through your bit, and don't go wrong again."

"Where are we?" asked Dave.

"Nearing Haskell's Land, I think," replied Jim. "We ought to slow down here, to drop a carriage for Penshill Bridge.

He walked to the window, lowered it, and looked out. Drawing back again, he said—

"Yes, we are near Haskell's, but not so near as I thought. Why—"

He stopped short, for, suddenly, to the utter amazement and discomfiture of himself and brother warder, the prisoner made a dash at the open window, through which he went head first, like a harlequin.

Both men made a grab at him, and Dave just succeeded in catching hold of the trousers worn by the convict, but the cloth gave way.

Down he went headlong upon the line, and Dave,

looking out, saw him lying in a heap upon the six-foot way.

Only for a moment or two he saw him, for the train was going round a curve, and speedily hid the form of the desperate man from sight.

"He's killed himself," said Dave, breathlessly.

"That's sure," said Jim; "but it won't right us. Signal the guard."

Dave thrust his head and shoulders from the window, waving his cap and shouting.

But the guard was busy sorting parcels or something, and saw nothing until the train had proceeded fully two miles on its way.

Then Dave's signal was seen by him, and knowing something was wrong he thrust out a red flag and the train stopped.

Hurried explanations followed, and the two warders alighting, ran back on the line, and presently arrived at the spot where the desperate Louis had thrown himself out.

They knew it by a patch of blood in the six-foot way, fresh and glistening in the sunlight; but that was all.

Whatever injury the convict might have suffered, he had succeeded in making his escape.

The two men looked around them over the wide stretch of land, and saw nobody but a labourer weeding or doing something of that nature in an adjacent field.

They went over to him to enquire if he had seen anything to guide them as to the direction Louis had taken. But he declared he had seen nothing.

He was a heavy, lumpish fellow, and only half comprehended what was said to him, so in weariness and disgust they turned away, and took the path across the field to the nearest police-station.

There all was done that the police could do. Men were despatched to scour the country, and telegrams sent around describing the convict.

It was all futile; their labour was in vain. Louis had escaped.

And now we come to the second scene.

This time it was on board the good ship Diadem, bound for China, but blown a long way out of her course by a series of heavy storms and contrary winds.

The crew on board was a mixed one, and for days there had been some demurring about the labour of the pumps and the double duty in other respects entailed by the adverse weather.

Many islands had been passed, and the crew advocated dropping anchor and taking a spell of rest.

But the captain refused to hear of it.

The ship would be days, or perhaps weeks, late in arriving at port as things were, and he would not permit anything to be done that promised further delay.

Among the crew was one man who, in a social sense, was undeniably superior to the rest of the men. He was a handsome, daring, reckless fellow, who had shipped just as the Diadem was about to sail, ostensibly to work his passage out to some friends in China.

He was one of many who are known to all seafaring men, and nothing was thought of his offer beyond that it was acceptable.

The Diadem was short-handed, and any help was better than none.

It was Louis Warrington, the escaped convict, who thus offered himself, and he soon became the "boss" of the forecastle.

Although not a practical sailor, he readily fell into his duties, and never exhibited any of the landsman's fear when going aloft.

He sang a good song, told a good story, and gave himself no airs.

Thus he succeeded in keeping on good terms with all the rough men around him, without exactly being one of them.

Before he had been a fortnight at sea, he was more their leader than the captain and he it was who led them into what was at first veiled revolt, and afterwards open mutiny.

It fairly broke out one morning when the ship, partly water-logged, came in sight of a wide stretch of mainland.

It seemed to be a fruitful, beautiful country, and the men, worn out with their exertions, wanted to rest.

Louis said nothing aloud; but he urged the grumblers on, and when the first mate ordered the men to their pumps, after a break of an hour or so, Louis bade them refuse.

"There are four officers and thirty men," he said; "why should the thirty be driven by this four like slaves?"

So when the mate gave the order not a man stirred.

The order was repeated with the same result.

Then the mate singled out one of the men and pointedly bade him go to his post.

He refused point blank, and the mate knocked him down.

Then the mutiny broke out.

The men had their knives, and a few had revolvers.

Some armed themselves with belaying pins. Louis, with a crowbar, led them on.

Briefly we will dwell on the terrible scene that followed.

The captain and other officers behaved like brave men, fighting to the last, and never yielding until they were overpowered.

Five mutineers lay dead upon the deck.

Several others were wounded; but the rest were mad with victory.

They cast their officers, wounded, but still living, overboard, and so gave them up to the sharks.

After that they broke into the spirit-room, and drank themselves first into a wild state, and then into stupidity. Through it all Louis Warrington kept his head straight.

His object was to get to some country where he might never be seen or recognised again.

Here was his opportunity.

Before him lay a fertile land, which looked as if it were inhabited, although there were no visible habitations or moving life on shore.

Inhabited or not, to that land he was going.

The first act was to bring the ship to, right in the eye of the wind, and then he lowered a boat.

Into this he cast several casks of biscuits and other food; also such arms and ammunition as he could find.

He even robbed the drunken comrades who had assisted him thus far.

Only a light wind was blowing, and the ship rocked idly on the deep, slowly drifting towards the shore, while he did this work.

At last all was ready, and with the captain's telescope he carefully scanned the shore.

No living being was in sight, and it seemed barely possible that mortal eye could have been a witness to the mutiny.

And now he entered on the last act of his plans, so carefully thought over, so coolly carried out.

Going below, he looked into the carpenter's room and secured his largest augur.

With this he descended into the hold, and drilled a hole through the bottom of the vessel below water-mark.

There were leaks enough in the good ship already; but the water spurted fiercely through the opening made, and practically sealed her doom.

Louis ran on deck, and looked around on the prostrate men.

If any compassion or remorse was in his soul, it was not exhibited in his face.

"They are little more than brutes," he said. "Why should I hesitate? Society will be my debtor for what I do this day."

He was about to leap down into the boat when a thought occurred to him.

His present attire was of the poorest for seagoing men, why should he not have something better?

He and the captain were about the same height, and the clothes of one would fit the other.

So down he dashed to the captain's cabin and speedily returned with an arm full of clothes, which he cast into the boat.

Then he loosened the rope, took the oars, and pulled

away at a safe distance, when he stopped to watch the
sinking ship.

She seemed to be slowly going down, but not by any
means so fast as he expected.

Half an hour passed, and she was still afloat, lying like
what she was, a water-logged ship upon the sea.

And now an unexpected factor introduced itself upon
the scene.

A dense fog came slowly up from the sea, obscuring all
things, and Louis, for his own sake, pulled for the
shore.

He reached it just as the leading mists was gathering
about him, and, hurriedly emptying the boat, he carried
the things inland, afterwards drawing up the boat as high
as he could from the sea.

He judged it was about high tide, and it would, therefore, so far, be perfectly safe.

To travel with such a fog about him was impossible,
and he lay down upon the soft sand to wait for it to lift.

But the wind suddenly dropped, and the fog remained.

Hour after hour through all the day it remained, until
the night came, and then it slowly rolled away, exhibiting
a sky studded with innumerable stars.

Whatever thoughts were in his head, he gave no physical
signs of them. Calmly this daring, wicked man, after partaking of food and smoking a pipe, lay down to sleep.

And he slept.

Slept until the morning came with its radiant sky,
showing him a land so rich in beauty that it seemed more
of Heaven than of earth.

To him that was of no great moment then.

He turned his eyes to the sea, and saw that the Diadem
was no longer in sight.

Of its fate he had no doubt, and his mind was at rest.

"Who will trace me now?" he cried, exultantly. "Who
will come here to drag me back to that horrible prison-
house?"

Returning to his boat, he tried to haul it higher up,
but it was too heavy, so he took up an axe he had brought
with him and deliberately cut it up, strewing the pieces

Down the rapids in the land of Jewels.

about the beach.

"Thus do I cut myself off from the old world," he said, "and enter on a new life. If alone, well; if in the companionship of savages, well too; if in the society of a strange, uncivilised people, better still.

The various things he had brought ashore with him were too numerous to be carried away, so he hid them inland in a hollow in the earth, covered the hole with branches he collected from trees a short distance away, and started inland, prospecting for a future home.

A mile from the shore the land rose up in undulating hills, and he made for one of the highest, climbing to its summit.

From there he looked around and beheld a scene or rather panorama of great beauty.

At his feet was a plain, through which a silvery river ran, and beyond the plain a line of mountains stretched right and left as far as he could see.

Everywhere there were signs of prodigal beauty, of richness and fertility of soil, and what was more to his taste just then, a number of habitations clustered together upon the bank of the river, but too far off to tell their precise nature, beyond that they were pretty structures mainly of wood.

Fully five miles they lay below, and after debating with himself, he resolved to time his arrival there so that he would have the darkness of night to cover him.

Then he could ascertain the nature of the inhabitants, and judge if it would be safe to reveal his presence.

Although he had said it would be well if he had to dwell there alone, he was already tiring of solitude.

It was that which had almost driven him mad in prison. He was neither by nature, association, nor aught else, fitted for the life of a hermit, and with impatience he watched the slow progress of the day.

He had brought sufficient food with him to satisfy the cravings of the time, also the pipe and tobacco which had become a familiar part of his "seafaring" life.

At last the sun was going down, and he started on his way.

CHAPTER VII.

LOUIS AND THE PATRIARCH—A BRIEF SKETCH OF THE
SURROUNDINGS—SCHEMES FOR THE FUTURE.

THE brief twilight of the clime found Louis near the
village, and darkness saw him crouching behind a pile of
logs outside.

During the day he had seen, in a casual hurried way,
men and women running about, but did not clearly make
out what they were like.

At the least they were not savages, for they were
dressed from head to heel, but their faces seemed too dark
for Europeans.

But with the night the houses were lighted up, and he
had a fair opportunity of judging what they were like.

Although he had never seen an Indian bungalow he
knew by reading something of their build, and these build-
ings were something of that nature, only more solid.

One building struck him as peculiar.

It was a square house upon a mound, and all round it was
a stockade—sound and strong—so he judged that he was
not altogether in a land of peace.

Here was evidence that there was need of refuge at
some particular time or season, but whether from men or
animals he had no means of knowing.

With the night there came a quietude inside the houses,
which he judged were something like a score in number.
All the inhabitants were within doors.

There was no regular street, for the habitations were
dotted about here and there, just as a child might put
down a number of toys upon the floor.

Selecting one Louis walked towards it, with cautious
steps, and reached a window which appeared at a distance
to be glazed with glass.

But it was not so—this apparent glass was horn, like
that which used to be fixed in the old-fashioned lanterns.

He put his ear to it and listened.

A subdued conversation was going on inside.

He could make out the voice of a man, evidently aged,
and that of a woman, who was young.

The language they were speaking was not only European but English.

Why should he hesitate any longer?

The door of the house, with its pretty trellised porch, was near the window.

He stepped lightly up and tapped.

Immediately the voices ceased.

After a few moments' stillness whispering ensued, and an inner door opened and shut.

He tapped again.

Then a small wicket in the door was opened, and he saw the face of a man with a long grey beard.

"Who is it?"

"A shipwrecked sailor," answered Louis; "an Englishman and a friend."

"A shipwrecked man," was the rejoinder. "How far have you come?"

"From the nearest point on the sea-shore," continued Louis; "we were driven out of our course—but—the story is a long one. I am faint and weary. Shall I pass on?"

"No," said the old man, as he threw open an iron door, letting a flash of light fall upon him. "Enter. It is the shipwrecked who can sympathise with a brother sufferer. My house is yours."

As he spoke he opened the outer door and admitted Louis, who found himself in an apartment, sparsely but comfortably furnished, lighted by a lamp swinging from the roof.

His host was a man of seventy years or more, but upright and keen of eye.

He was clad in rough home-spun—a long coat, trousers, and boots; in his hand he held a rifle.

"We have sometimes to be wary of strangers," he said. "See, my friend. Clara, all is well. It is another friend."

Then from an inner room emerged a girl of surpassing beauty, who welcomed Louis with quiet grace.

"A friend came from the river but a few days ago," said the old man, "and now we have another from the sea."

"Friends from the river?" said Louis, with a puzzled face.

"Yes; or I may say from the jaws of death," said the old man; "and now it strikes me that he is something like you. Come and see him? There is no harm. He has had the fever, and is sleeping—having touched the land of recovery. Clara, spread the table for our latest friend? Sir, will you follow me?"

The old man hurried through the doorway by which Clara had just appeared, and Louis followed him.

The inner room was smaller, and fitted as a bed-chamber.

On a couch lay a young man sleeping, the light of a lamp on a table by his side shining on his face.

Louis stopped short with a catching of his breath, and then took another step forward and stooped down, gazing with eager eyes, at the sick man's face.

It was his brother Hal !

Louis was so taken aback by the sight of Hal that for a minute or more he uttered not a word—indeed, he could hardly realise the reality of the thing.

It would have amazed any living man to have thus been thrown into the society of a brother in a strange, far-off land, where there could have been no reasonable hope of their meeting.

But life is full of strange surprises.

There is a divinity that shapes our ends,
Rough hew them how we will.

The old man looked closely at Louis, somewhat puzzled by the dumbfounded expression of his face.

"You are pained," he said. "The sight of your fellow-countryman has overcome you?"

"Yes, yes," said Louis, hurriedly. "Has he been ill long?"

"About fourteen days," was the reply; "but the worst is over. He is in the sleep of convalescence, and will be better when he wakes."

"He will know—you again?" said Louis.

The word "me" was on his tongue, but he checked it just in time.

"No," said the old man, faintly smiling. "He will not know me nor anyone, for he was rescued from the rapids in a state of insensibility—so bruised and beaten about that that we had little hope of his life. His companion was wounded, and we thought he was dead; but he, strange to say, was the first to get well."

"Who is his companion?" asked Louis.

"A man who calls himself a servant, and acts like an attached friend," replied the old man. "He calls himself Grip."

"And where is he?" calmly asked Louis.

"Away with my son, Felix," replied the old man. "They are scouting in the hills, for there is a report that the Tourgovons are coming hither. But, come, you are weary, and must eat. While you partake of your evening meal I can tell you of many things that may interest you."

They returned to the outer room, where Clara had prepared supper for Louis.

There were many unexpected dainties spread out before him—well-cooked meat, brown, crisp bread of some sort, and even a vase of flowers; but Louis had little appetite.

For a shipwrecked sailor he ate very sparingly, while Clara sat back, busy with some needlework, and the old man briefly sketched the history of his strange settlement.

It was formed mostly of his family and relatives, who were Russians, and had fled from their country to escape a threatened banishment to Siberia.

The whole family came away in a steamer chartered from England by sympathising, wealthy friends.

Their family name was Menlonvitz, and the old man was the Patriarch of his people.

On board the same vessel was another refugee family, named Tourgovon, who were avowed Nihilists, which the Menlonvitches were not.

The Tourgovons had a lot of Tartar blood in their veins; they were wild and almost savage men.

Oil and water will not mix, and these two families, though one in the point of being refugees, could not fraternise for long.

They were landed on the shores of the fertile, lovely

land in which Louis found them—a part of the great dark continent of Africa, out of the line of the ordinary explorer, and for awhile pitched their tents or huts in company.

But it was soon clear that they could not long remain together.

The natives were a peaceful people, and Gavril Tourgovon tyrannised over them. Though a refugee from a tyrant, he proved to be one himself, and sought to make some of the people slaves.

In fact, he did so, and withdrew to a spot about fifteen miles away, where he had been for seven years.

"It is a land of plenty—a paradise," said the old man, "but not of peace. Gavril Tourgovon is a fierce, unholy man, and his son is wilder still ; and yet to think that he should dare to—"

The old man stopped short and looked at Clara. Louis raised his eyes to her face, and saw that her cheeks were flushed.

Therein lay the gist of what the patriarch had left unsaid.

Adrian Tourgovon wanted Clara for a wife, and the proposal was offensive to her and to her friends.

"There is a feud between us," said the Patriarch, "and at times we have to take refuge in a small fort we have constructed. Happily there is a scarcity of arms among us on both sides."

Then he told Louis of the strange contrast between the natives on this side of the river and those on the other.

Across the water lay a wide stretch of land of many hundred square miles, filled with horrible tribes, that of Peruquio being the best.

His people were bad enough, being cruel at all times and cannibals at a pinch, but they were civilised beings compared to some of the hideous tribes that lived like hordes of wild beasts in the vast forests that could be seen in the daytime from the higher ground like a line of clouds in the horizon.

"Sometimes we see them on the opposite shore," said the patriarch. "They come down like beasts to dabble in the water and drink, but the river is swift and strong.

They swim very little, and make no attempt to cross."

"Having no boats?" said Louis, dreamily, with his eyes on Clara, whose beauty grew upon him.

It acted upon his ardent nature like a spell.

"They had our canoe," said the patriarch, "which originally belonged to us   One of my family "—here his voice trembled a little—" went up above the falls one day, and never returned. The canoe, garnished and ornamented by savage hands, came back with Hal—Grip says it is his name. He found it on the shore. I need not tell you his story. He will relate it to you anon; for surely you will be friends, being of the same country, and somewhat alike? You might be brothers."

"I have no brother," replied Louis, serenely.

"I like the English people," said the patriarch, musing. "My dear wife—sainted now—was of English birth. Hence my daughter's name. We have always cultivated your tongue, too, and use it in preference to our own."

Louis had now finished supper, and Clara cleared the table, doing the humble office with a grace that deprived it of all that was commonplace.

"With a girl like that," thought Louis, "and a few companions, one might be happy here."

It was getting late, and his host offered to show him to his chamber

"Felix's room," he said; "he will not need it to-night or to-morrow, as he will not return until the following day."

Everything about the simple house was very neat, although there was evidence of wear, partly concealed by neat repairing and mending.

Louis lay down to rest on the bed provided for him, but not to sleep.

His mind was filled with a whirpool of thought—bitter and pleasing commingled.

If Hal had not been in that house he might have stayed there, or at the little settlement at least, a welcome guest. Clara might have been wooed and won—but why speculate?

THAT would never be, for he must away to-morrow early, unless his brother did not recover, as the patriarch hoped.

And even if he did not there was Grip.

No;—he must go and at once, and his next step must be to throw in his lot with the Tourgovons.

He had faith in his daring spirit, and it was possible that he might eventually become their leader.

They lacked arms, and he had some hidden away, and would immediately be a welcome addition to their strength.

In a few hours of sleeplessness he had mapped out a career which would suit his fast developing lawless tastes, and he was eager to begin it at once.

He could not sleep—why should he lie idle there?

The dawn would soon show him the direction of the hills, and thither he would wend his way, and the Tourgovon settlement could not be hard to find.

He arose, dressed himself, and softly stole out of the house where he had been so hospitably received without one word of thanks or grateful thought.

The light of the stars was waning, and day was at hand. Peaceful and silent was the little settlement, soon to awake to the business of the day, and ere long to be roused to action by the coming of foes.

Louis stole outside the village, and waited for the first ray of light to guide him on his road.

It came in due course, and showed him the hills like large waves in the horizon, and thither he turned his footsteps.

"Sweet Clara," he said, with a backward motion of the hand towards the patriarch's house, "I leave you now, but I shall come back again."

He had a pair of pistols with him, which he carried concealed in his pocket.

Drawing them out he examined the charges carefully.

"The Tourgovons may not prove amicable," he muttered, "in that case I must teach them a lesson. Hal, my brother, you were ever in my way. *I hate you.* Oh! darling of our mother, who saw so little in me. Hal, for your own sake I trust you will not stand between me and that charming Clara. Pshaw! Louis, what fool you are.

You are not a boy to look and love, and yet it seems to me that in this outlandish spot you have met your fate."

He lingered for a moment, loth to go ; but his inability to stay thrust itself upon him, and, with a muttered anathema hurled at the head of unconscious brother, he tore himself away.

CHAPTER VIII.

CLARA AND HAL—ENCOUNTER WITH WILD ADRIAN— THE ATTACK AT NIGHT.

WHEN the light had come, and the settlement awoke to the duties of the day, Clara was among the first to be up and doing.

The patriarch, notwithstanding his age, was an early riser, and, while Clara was busy with arranging the living-room, he went in to see Hal.

He was awake, lying quite passive, happy, and with an air of luxurious ease, surveying the fittings of his room.

The entrance of his host, of whom he had no previous knowledge, roused him from his serenity, and he made an effort to rise.

"Do not exert yourself," said the old man, "you have been very ill."

He drew a small bottle from his pocket and, watched by the wondering but silent Hal, poured a small portion of its contents in a cup that stood on a chair by the bed-side.

Having added water, he gave it to the patient.

"Drink," he said ; "it will revive you."

Hal complied with the docility of a child, and, refreshed, he was able to listen to the patriarch, who told the story of his timely rescue.

How he had been seen by Felix, who was out in search of game, coming down the rapids, and after the over-turning of the canoe was tossed about like a cork until Felix, who plunged in, was able to rescue him.

Grip, to a certain extent, needed no rescue, he having been fairly thrown ashore, and lay there until help could be obtained from the settlement.

The canoe was also saved, having got wedged between two rocks, from whence it was extricated by the settlers.

Hal was grateful, and more than pleased to hear that Grip was alive. Towards Felix he felt the deepest gratitude, for life, with all its troubles, cares, and humiliations, he desired, like the rest of us, to keep.

The greatest revelation of all was the first sight of Clara, who presently brought in his breakfast.

She seemed to him to possess a beauty that was more than earthly; her gentle bearing charmed and her sweet voice thrilled him.

Ere the day was out he was able to sit up a little and talk with the patriarch.

He told him of his past, of his broken home, but not of his brother's sin and shame.

The past, so far as Louis was concerned, he wished buried ten thousand fathoms deep.

The next morning Grip and Felix returned, and Hal's eyes were gladdened by the sight of his faithful servitor, and his rescuer from the rapids.

Between Felix and Hal a friendship was immediately formed.

They were about the same age, but Felix was of a different type.

He had the undemonstrative bearing of the Russian, saying little and thinking a great deal.

He repudiated all idea of merit in what he had done.

"It is nothing," he said. "Any man would have done as much and more, and forget all about it the next day."

Grip was in the seventh heaven on his own account, but a little more about his friend.

He and Felix had discovered that preparations were being made for an attack upon somebody, but, of course, could not tell if it were to be the settlement or one of the peaceful tribes.

Wild horses had been seen about for the first time, and Adrian Tourgovon had secured one, which he was observed to be breaking in.

"A few horses would be useful to us," said Felix.

It seemed clear the attack threatened was not to be upon the settlement, for days passed, and the men on the other side of the hills made no sign.

Day and night a watch was kept, all able-bodied men, and they were not many, taking turn at sentry duty.

Hal recovered rapidly, and was soon able to walk in the open air.

Clara became his companion on two occasions, and the old, old story began to unfold itself.

Love, the little god, aimed his darts at their hearts, and hit home.

But not a word was said.

Hal respected the hospitality he had received, and he also asked himself of what avail would it be for him to speak.

But it was a very pleasant time for him and Clara too.

One morning Hal walked out alone, and, thinking of Clara, unconsciously wandered away from the settlement inland.

Nobody had warned him against doing so, for it was an accepted maxim that nobody was to go abroad alone.

He was aroused from a dream by hearing the pattering of a horse's feet, and, looking up, he saw a stranger galloping towards him.

From the description he had heard of Adrian Tourgovon, the peril of his position flashed upon him.

Adrian was riding straight at him, carrying at the charge a long lance, made in imitation of those carried by Cossacks of his native land.

There was mischief in his eyes as he bore straight at Hal, without uttering a cry of warning.

Afar off—behind him—Hal saw the form of a man watching the scene.

Brief as this glimpse was that he caught of the distant watcher the form seemed familiar.

However, he had no time to look closely at him. Adrian commanded his attention.

Hal did not lose his head.

Quietly he awaited the onslaught of the grim, determined ruffian, who bore down upon him with the keen air of a hunter in sight of a quarry.

Not until the last moment, when Adrian was fairly upon him, did Hal flinch.

The lance, indeed, was within a few inches of his heart, when he leapt aside, and dexterously grasped the weapon a foot or so from the point.

He had got back some of his old strength, and with all his might he endeavoured to wrench it from his would-be assassin. The result of his onslaught so surprised Adrian that he lost his grip upon the rough saddle he rode upon, and not leaving hold of the lance he was twisted in his seat and rolled off the horse.

He fell to the ground with a force that threatened to dislocate every bone in his body; and the horse, freed from his grasp, snorted with a sense of renewed freedom, and galloped away out of sight.

Hal, with the lance in his hand, walked up to the prostrate Adrian, who was writhing on the ground with pain.

Just for a moment it was in Hal's heart to kill him, but he was not made of the stuff that leads a man to strike a prostrate foe.

He gave way to his generous impulses and spared him. The fruits of this nobility of heart were to come by-and-bye.

"Who are you?" demanded Hal; "and what have I done to you that you should seek my life?"

"Take mine," was the sullen answer, "and waste no words in idle chattering."

"No," returned Hal. "Can you rise? Give me your hand."

"What! will you give a hand to the man who seeks your life?"

"Yes—as you are; but when we meet again I may call you to account for what you did to-day."

"I cannot take your hand," said Adrian.

He did not say why, but slowly rose and carefully felt himself all over.

The result extracted from him a grunt of satisfaction.

"Nothing smashed," he said.

Then he looked at Hal again.

"You are a MAN," he said, and, turning round, limped away.

Hal remained watching him a while, but he did not look back, and then, with the lance in his hand, strolled back to the settlement.

Ere he reached it he saw Grip and Felix coming out to meet him.

They stared at the lance, and he laughingly told him of his "little adventure."

"That brute Adrian!" said Felix. "He loves killing for killing's sake."

For all that they wondered why he should set upon a stranger without a word.

Now up to that time nothing had been said to Hal about the arrival and secret departure of Louis.

The patriarch and his family naturally considered they had been very scurvily treated by a stranger, or had been intruded upon by a spy from their foes.

But now it leaked out, so that Hal heard a description of his brother which he easily recognised.

Nevertheless, he could not credit that it was Louis.

The reader knows how he came there, but to Hal it was an inscrutable mystery.

He had little time to speculate upon it, for that evening the scout came in with the tidings that the Tourgovons were coming over the hills in force, bearing straight upon the settlement.

Then preparations were made to receive them.

A few arms which the settlers possessed were got out, with Hal's and Grip's rifles, which had been securely placed inside the canoe, and had been found there.

The rust had been cleaned off by Grip, and the whole thing put properly in order.

The few rounds of ammunition possessed by the two adventurers had also been carefully dried.

The little fort or stockade which had been mainly erected as a last resort from savages had now to be utilised as a place of safety from white men—fellow-countrymen !

And, worst of all, one brother was advancing as a foe

to slay another brother !

Stealthily under the cover of darkness the Tourgovons and their following drew near.

They came on foot, for the one horse they possessed had been lost that day.

Where was the rider? Not with the advancing party.

Adrian was the only one of the band who remained behind, declaring that he was unable to move.

But side by side with Gavril Tourgovon marched Louis Warrington, with no compunction about the work he was engaged in, and no misgivings as to the result.

He was sure that the doom of the Menlonvitch family was sealed.

On, with stealthy, cat-like steps, they drew near the settlement.

All was still and dark.

"Asleep !" muttered Louis to Gavril, and quietly they surrounded the house of the patriarch.

"Be sure not to hurt the girl," was the final whispered order, and a man advanced with a crowbar to break in the door.

Then from the rear the report of a rifle was heard, and Gavril Tourgovon, who was standing beside Louis, leaped up without a cry, and fell forward on his face.

CHAPTER IX.

THE FAILURE OF THE NIGHT ATTACK—LOUIS AND ADRIAN—WHO SHALL BE LEADER?

THERE was a great commotion among the Tourgovons as they scattered to find a hiding-place.

Louis Warrington alone did not fly.

Quick of thought and brave of heart, he saw his opportunity and embraced it.

By one simple act he established his ascendency over the Tourgovon family.

Instead of flying like the rest, he stooped over the form of the fallen man, and ascertained that he was dead.

Then, taking up the body in his arms, he carried it behind the house of the patriarch, and gently laid it down.

Half-a-dozen men were skulking there, and to them he said—

"You have lost your leader—I will be your leader now.   Follow me."

But they would not stir.

"The Menlonvitches are well armed and under cover," they said.   "Our surprise has been turned against us."

Louis did not argue with them.

He saw that the game was up for that night, at least; and with a muttered anathema on their cowardice, he bade them take up their dead chief and carry him home.

"Make a circuit out of the reach of the fire," Louis said.

For himself, he once more showed in the open, and called upon the other men in hiding to come forth.

"This is Menlonvitch hospitality!" he said.   "Ah! we will reply to it by-and-bye."

The sneering jest was so common a thing with him that he could not resist the uttering of one even at that time.

Walking near to the little fort, he cried out—

"We came as friends to-night—we leave as enemies. Marvel at nothing we may do next."

With this lie he left them and sauntered off, saved by the clemency of a brother who would not shed his blood.

The disappointed Tourgovons, in scattered form, hastened homewards in the darkness.

They knew their way, and Nature had pretty well defined the road over the hills.

Louis Warrington was one of the first to reach their lair —a sweet spot in the valley beyond, where the palm-trees grew in abundance, and wild fruits and gorgeous flowers were the weeds of the land.

On the banks of a small tributary there they had raised their huts, and in one of these sat Adrian, brooding.

The night had almost past, and he had not slept.

Rough and violent by nature, he had still something of the heart of a man in him, and the purposed slaughter of that night had been distasteful to his feelings.

Against Louis Warrington he already felt a keen animosity.

He instinctively felt that the English outlaw had come there to *rule*, and a usurpation of this family power Adrian resented.

His meditations were interrupted by the door being thrown open and Louis entering.

He drew a rough seat up to the table by which Adrian was sitting, and cast his hat down upon it.

"What sort of men do you call your followers?" Louis asked.

"Good men," was the short answer.

"Curs!" said Louis, between his teeth. "They fled —fairly bolted—at the first shot, simply because it happened to take effect. The old patriarch and his lot had taken refuge in the fort. They seem to have expected us."

"Who fell?" asked Adrian.

"One whom you can ill spare," said Louis—"your father!"

Adrian started to his feet, and uttered a loud cry of anguish.

"It is useless howling over it," said Louis, roughly. "A man can die but once, and I believe your father was a brave man; but he was no commander—no leader."

Adrian glanced angrily at Louis, and put his hand into his belt.

"You killed him!" he cried.

And then with another cry he sprang upon Louis.

The onslaught was not expected, and Louis was borne to the ground. But he was not daunted or dismayed.

Cool as if engaged in a mere friendly bout he seized Adrian by the waist, and, locked together, they rolled about the floor of the hut until Louis was uppermost.

Then he saw that his antagonist had a knife in his grasp, and wrenched it from him.

In another moment he would have used it in retaliation, but there were voices and footsteps outside and he refrained.

Rising, and placing the knife in his own pocket, he said—

"Get up, you mad fool! Ask any of your people who killed your father."

The men who were the bearers of the body now brought it in on a rough bier made of the branches of trees.

A silence fell upon the scene, and the bereaved Adrian, with clasped hands, bent over the still form.

"Dead!" was all he said.

It was only one word, but volumes could not have expressed more anguish.

However rough and lawless he and his father might have been they had loved each other.

Louis stole softly out and paced up and down outside the hut. A few minutes later the bearers of the corpse went out, and father and son—the living and the dead—were left alone.

The tired adventurers sought their respective places of repose, but Louis did not attempt to sleep.

He and Adrian were the only two who did not close their eyes that night.

In the early morning Adrian came forth and saw Louis walking up and down with his hands behind him.

For a few moments they stood and looked at each other —Adrian fierce and bitter, Louis calm and insolent.

"My father being dead," said Adrian, "I am ruler here."

"Indeed!" replied Louis.

"I inherit the position by right of birth," said Adrian, "and my commands will have to be obeyed."

Louis raised his eyebrows and lightly laughed.

"So will mine," he said.

"Yours?" exclaimed Adrian. "Who are you that you should dare to attempt to usurp that power? It was yesterday that you came here a wandering outcast. We took you in and treated you as a friend, and now, like the viper in the fable that the fool warmed in his bosom, you would turn and sting us."

"In a land like this," said Louis, "the strongest rule, and no other. It is no question of right or of birth, or anything else, but might. Call the men together—you have a signal."

Adrian put his hands to his mouth and uttered a cry that echoed far away.

It was the signal of alarm—the calling to a muster roll of the Tourgovons.

They came hurrying out of their rough huts—a band of twenty odd, wild-eyed men, each grasping such weapons as he possessed.

Adrian's calm demeanour reassured them.

"There is no foe near," he said. "You have been summoned here to say if I am not your leader now that my father is no more—for here is an accursed stranger who seeks to usurp my place."

The men looked at Louis, who smiled sarcastically.

"If they choose you," he said, "they have no leader. Here, you men, you want someone with courage, daring and resolute, at the head of you. I offer myself—you need me."

The men looked at him from under their shaggy eyebrows, remembering how cool he had been the night before, but said not a word.

"Get you from here !" said Adrian to Louis.

"I refuse to go !" was the reply.

"Men," cried Adrian, fiercely, "remove him !"

Louis backed a little, so as to get them all in front of him, and then, drawing a pistol, said, quietly—

"I will kill the first man who touches me. But what need is there of wrangling ? You say you are leader. I say I will be leader. Let it be a question of might between you and me. I will wrestle with you for the supremacy—the first two falls—and he who is last down is to yield to the other."

In appearance Adrian was the better and the stronger man. Louis looked quite frail beside him.

"Let it be so," said Adrian, as he proceeded to pull off his outer coat.

He had no doubt the victory would be on his side.

The men in a sullen way awaited the issue of the struggle.

It did not concern them so very much after all. As for interfering, they did not think it would be safe to put themselves in antagonism to the evil and daring stranger.

Louis threw off nothing but his hat, and with a jaunty smile advanced to do battle for the position of ruler of this half-savage band.

The two men closed, and then, as if he were a child, Adrian was thrown heavily to the ground.

"I was barely prepared," he gasped.

"In my land," said Louis, "you do not require a week for reflection ; but if it is not fair let us to it again."

For a second time they closed, and Louis, after a pause, asked—

"Are you ready?"

"Yes," was the answer.

Aud then, as if he were a toy, Adrian was lifted and thrown over the left shoulder of Louis.

He fell with a crash, as if every bone in his body were broken, and lay still.

It was skill as much as strength that triumphed, and the victory had its due effect.

The spectators did not cheer.

If Adrian had triumphed they might have indulged in some outburst peculiar to their race, but with Louis triumphant they were grimly silent.

As a born leader of men he had secured their vassalage.

Louis bent over Adrian and heard his breathing. Then ne examined his limbs and found they were not broken.

"Take him to the river," he said, "and throw some water over him. He will soon revive. If he is not satisfied then I will try another bout with him."

CHAPTER X.

A BRIEF SPELL OF PEACE—THE WILD MEN ON THE SHORE—THE ANACONDA SNAKE—BURNING HUTS.

THE retreat of the Tourgovons was unexpected by the Melonvitches, who in the dusk did not see who it was that had fallen.

It was Felix who fired the shot, using his father's rifle.

Hal and Grip stood ready to use their weapons if the

foe should really attempt to carry the stockade.

The little hut in the stockade was bullet-proof, and in it the few women and children of the settlement had been placed, Clara alone excepted.

She insisted upon remaining outside, to act, if occasion arose, as one of the defending party.

"Better to die," she said to Hal, "than become the captive of the Tourgovons."

The retreat of the foe was at first looked upon as a *ruse*, but after the lapse of an hour Grip undertook to go out and scout around. Hal would not let him go alone, so they went together.

In half an hour they returned with the good tidings that the enemy had retreated.

Still it was not considered safe to come out in the dark and they passed the night in the little fort.

At dawn they came out, and returned to their homes.

And now the system of watching the fort was resumed with a startling result.

Their very first scout returned with the tidings that the Tourgovons had disappeared.

Even their huts had been pulled to pieces and cast down.

One thing was noticed by the scout, and that was a grave over which a rough wooden cross had been placed.

Grip, unasked, and without giving notice of his intentions, went out to inspect that grave, and came back with the tidings that the words "Gavril Tourgovon" had been rudely cut upon it.

A week elapsed.

A happy week for Hal, days of peace all too soon to come to an end.

No sign of the foe—and nothing to disturb them beyond the arrival of some dwarfish men on the other side of the river, who gibbered and capered about for awhile, and then went back to the wood.

They were awful-looking beings, as ugly as one ever saw in a dream.

Their monkeyish actions terrified the women and children, and infuriated the men.

But nothing was done.

Ammunition was scarce, and it would not do to waste it, so unharmed they capered and grinned and went their way.

Gradually there stole over the settlement a sense of security.

The men went out singly or in twos to set traps for game in the woods around, in one of which, about four miles north, a rough wooden hut was erected for the hunters to pass the night, if they thought it necessary.

In this place Grip and Hal went one evening to see if they could get a shot at some deer that had been seen grazing about.

They were a very keen nosed species, scenting the coming of a man at an incredible distance, and hitherto all attempts to capture or kill one had failed.

Pits had been dug, and traps set without avail, and it occurred to Hal that by means of a few pierced holes in the hut a shot might be got at one as the drove went by.

So to the hut they resolved to go, thinking little of it, and having no fears.

Clara, however, was rather sad.

"It is foolish of me," she said, "but I feel it wrong to let you go."

"What is there to feel?" said Hal. "We have no foes in the place. Our enemies have disappeared."

"Yes, I know," she said; "it is weak and childish of me to heed a dream. Go!"

"What was your dream?" he asked.

"Nothing. I will not tell you," she replied.

No words of love had been spoken yet, nor was there need of them. The love that was in their hearts was in their eyes.

All in the settlement could see it, and all approved.

Hal and Grip departed, the former not without a sense of heaviness.

He was disposed to laugh at all dreams, as others have laughed until the awakening comes.

They reached the hut and shut themselves in. After cutting loopholes they lay close until the morning.

Before there was any real daylight they were up and watching for the expected game.

Slowly increased the light, and then Grip marked something like a coil of rope not far from the door.

He drew Hal's attention to it, but neither could clearly make out what it was until it moved.

It was a big snake, the first they had seen in the place. They had not even heard of such a thing.

This was an unwelcome discovery, and this reptile, as it reared its flat, venomous head, had a very angry look about it.

"It is twenty feet long," said Grip, "if it is an inch."

"More," replied Hal. "It is coiled very close, and lies in a small hollow. If I mistake not, it is one of the species called anaconda; they grow to an enormous length. Travellers have written of them being ninety or a hundred feet in length."

"That one is long enough for me," said Grip. "Look at it now!"

The snake had raised its head; the long, thin tongue, the "feeler" of its genus, was darting in and out with a rapidity of motion that was very striking.

Suddenly there was a pattering of hoofs, and the reptile's head rose higher in the air.

"The deer!" cried Hal.

Forgetting for the moment all else, he and Grip got their rifles ready, each at a loophole on either side of the hut.

On came the deer at a furious pace, evidently scared by something.

They went by like a succession of flashes of light.

Hal fired at one and saw it spring up; but it was not killed outright, and fled on.

The snake struck at one of them and missed.

Two seconds later and the herd had gone by, and the snake, uncoiling itself, went in pursuit.

A vain pursuit, no doubt, for the time; but by steadily keeping in the track, the reptile might by-and-bye stealthily come upon them when grazing.

Hal threw open the door of the hut and darted out.

"I have wounded one, Grip," he said. "See, there's the trail of blood."

"Better let the snake have it," said Grip, quietly. "I don't like the look of that critter."

"Not if I can help it," said Hal.

He set out on the trail, but he had barely moved half-a-dozen steps when an ejaculation of dismay burst from Grip.

Then, indeed, the cause of the stampede was revealed.

Travelling through the wood at an enormous rate for a reptile came a large snake, compared to which the one they had recently seen was an infant.

Petrified, the two men stood for a moment, taken quite aback by the sight of such a monster.

The raised head and quick motion of a tongue fully eighteen inches long, increased its formidable appearance.

Of such things Hal had read and doubted—now he believed.

The snake approached them, and death had surely come to them then but for the fact that the huge anaconda was bent upon getting at the deer, and was not to be turned aside by less tempting prey.

It hissed at them as if in warning not to get into its path again, and then, glittering and sparkling in the morning light, disappeared in the wood.

"Master Hal," gasped Grip, "did you see it?"

"What a question, Grip!" replied Hal.

"Then it is here, and I didn't fancy it?"

"No, Grip, it's real enough. What a horrible sight! And I was a fool not to shoot it. But it only shows that the best of us may be unnerved. It was an *unnatural* sight!"

"Maybe, Master Hal," said Grip, philosophically. "We shall get used to 'em by-and-bye."

"Grip," said Hal, "with such a monster here life would not be safe. While the anaconda can get a wild creature for its food, well; but, failing that, it will take man, woman, or child."

"We oughtn't to ha' let it pass, Master Hal."

" Let us try to make amends for a moment's weakness by going after it."

"Master Hal, I'm ready."

The trail of the wounded deer was easily followed, and this was sufficient to guide them on the track of the two anacondas.

They had not far to go.

The deer had not run more than a hundred yards, and then fallen.

The first anaconda had overtaken it and enveloped it in its folds.

Then came the second and larger reptile, which in its turn enfolded it, crushing both the deer and the smaller member of its own species.

Hal and Grip arrived in time to become spectators of a terrible and loathsome scene.

The smaller anaconda was writhing in the embrace of the larger one as it contracted its folds, crushing the deer into a shapeless mass.

As a rope might be put around a thing and drawn, so it drew in its body, tightening its deadly grip to prepare its food for swallowing and digesting.

Intent on its work, it did not see the two men approach, and Hal took steady aim at its raised head.

Sharp and clear the rifle rang out its deadly note, and the head of the monster anaconda was shattered.

It was not dead, but it at once relaxed its hold, and writhed about the ground like the python we read of in the heathen fable when tortured by the arrows of Apollo.

The dying throes of the sinuous creature compelled our two friends to retreat to a little distance, for the tail beat the ground and struck the trees, dashing off some of the smaller branches, while its whole length quivered and throbbed with pain.

Gladly would Hal have put it out of its misery if he could, but there was no part of it where a shot, so far as he knew, would tell with vital effect.

So it twisted and writhed for a quarter of an hour or more—to the watchers it seemed treble that time—and its force began to yield.

Its contortions sobered down and finally ceased. The huge creature lay full length in the forest—dead.

And hard by was the deer and the lesser anaconda, a crushed and shapeless mass.

Who would have cared to linger by such a scene?

Already swarms of flies and other insects were settling down to play the part of Nature's scavengers by removing the carcases in infinitesimal portions.

Anon some of the lower beasts of prey would appear on the scene.

"Let us go, Grip," said Hal. "I have had enough of it for to-day."

So had Grip.

He was a brave man, but there are certain things that overwhelm the stoutest, and such a scene as this was one of them.

They walked away, and coming to a cool spring, drank of its limpid waters to refresh themselves.

Both had food with them, but neither cared to eat.

A few minutes' more took them clear of the forest, and then they saw something that was even worse than the awful struggles of the anaconda.

Ahead of them lay the settlement—ON FIRE.

Every hut and house was burning, and in such a way as showed they had been on fire for an hour or more.

Nobody could be seen endeavouring to quench the flames.

What could that mean?

The dreadful sickness that comes over a good, kind-hearted man when he feels apprehensive about others came over Hal.

Grip's cheeks were pale again, and his eager eyes were fixed enquiringly on the flames.

"What has happened, Master Hal?"

"I don't know," was the faint response. "I fear much. Oh! Grip, this is worse than all."

He started forward at a run, and Grip followed him.

With a few feet between them they fairly tore across the intervening ground.

As they drew nearer there was a prospect of their worst

apprehensions being fulfilled.

First they saw the form of a man lying at full length upon the ground, so still that there could be no doubt that he was dead.

Then another, and then a woman with a child in her arms.

All so dreadfully still.

And the huts, only a few hours before filled with life, were being fast reduced to ashes.

It was a calm morning, not a breath of wind ruffled the air.

The flames rose skyward, with crowns of smoke that slowly spread out thinner and thinner until lost in the sunlight.

Swiftly and silently Hal traversed the village, counting the bodies that lay scattered about.

All dead but three.

He could find no trace of the patriarch, Clara, or Felix.

It appeared, then, that they had been made captives.

But by whom?

And while he asked himself this question his eye alighted on a stick thrust into the ground a short way from the houses.

The top of it had been split, and a strip of paper thrust into the cleft thus made.

It was clear that it had been put there for somebody, and that somebody, he feared, was himself.

He walked up, and, removing the paper, read the following words scrawled in pencil—

"*My good, ever good, brother Hal,—Wish self and bride long life and happiness. Drink to us, if only from the flowing river.—Your loving brother,* "LOUIS."

"So he *is* here," said Hal, between his teeth, "and with the old sardonic spirit unchanged."

He stood quite still, with his eyes ahead, wondering, in a dazed, despairing way, what freak of nature had made this man his brother.

So unlike the father and mother to whom he owed existence.

Hal's father had been a careless and a dissipated man, but he was of generous disposition, and would never have done aught dishonourable.

Mrs. Warrington was one of the gentlest of women.

Oh ! it was strange, incomprehensible, but, alas ! too true.

Grip touched Hal on the arm.

" You've something there that's bad, Master Hal ?" he said.

" Read it," was the husky reply.

The writing was bold and clear, and Grip, albeit no scholar, read it easily.

" What's this ?" he exclaimed.   " What put it into his head to take her away ?"

" Oh ! Grip," said Hal, with a sob, " he knows somehow that I love, and this is another instance of his strange, unnatural hatred.   Grip, what shall I do ?"

" Try to find him, Master Hal."

" If we met I might kill him.   No ; I must fly away, for the blood of a brother must never be on my head !"

" And then you must leave that poor, purty dove to her fate ?" said Grip, sadly.

A choking feeling came over Hal.

It was indeed so.

If he obeyed the better promptings of his nature and fled away from his brother, he must leave Clara to the mercies of his sardonic, inhuman brother.

No ; he could not do that.

And was there not, in addition, the fact that Felix and his aged father were captives also ?

Hal could not leave them.

In this strange and bitter turn of events he must do his duty and sink SELF !

" The struggle is none of my seeking," he said, with clasped hands.   " I have resisted until now all feud with him, but I must e'en be at war with my brother, whether I will or no.   Louis, look to it !   The consequences of this unnatural struggle be on your head.   It is your work, not mine !"

Turning to Grip he said, with a calmness that was

terrible—

"I go from here, not to seek a brother, but one who is by choice a foe to his fellow man. Like some officer of justice who is commanded to arrest and bring to punishment a near kinsman, so do I obey the promptings of a just spirit and go in search of my brother Louis."

"Oh! Master Hal," said Grip, "it is very bitter!"

"But it must be borne," said Hal. "Come, their trail must be easy to find. Find it, and lead the way. I will follow wherever it leads, and if I rescue Clara the end of it may, for aught I care, be death!"

CHAPTER XI.

LOUIS WARRINGTON AS CAPTAIN OF A BAND—A STRANGE FIND.

LOUIS WARRINGTON had so far played his cards well. He was master of the band of ruffians, the majority of whom were of the Tourgovon family.

The way he had dispensed of Adrian effectually settled the question of leadership.

After the deadly grapple between them, and the fall of Adrian, the defeated son of Gavriel Tourgovon had his choice of remaining as under-officer to Louis or going away.

He chose the latter course, and without a friend he set out for the hills and was seen no more.

Then Louis proceeded to play a cunning game.

He removed his quarters to a quiet vale among the hills, and then lay close until he had lulled the Menlonvitches into a feeling of security.

It was done, and on the night Hal went to the wood Louis descended upon the village.

He came so stealthily that his presence was not suspected until too late.

Some never knew of his coming, for they were murdered as they slept.

And those awakened, being isolated from their fellows, could only offer a feeble resistance.

Three only were spared.

The patriarch, Clara, and Felix.

The latter would assuredly have been slain but that Louis desired to curry favour with Clara.

He wished to be in a position to say—

"The nearest of your kith and kin I spared for your sake!"

He desired to win Clara's love.

It was a mad idea after the atrocities he had been guilty of; but Louis thought he knew something of women.

He believed they were to be won under any circumstances, provided the wooer went the right way to work.

With their arms bound he led his captives away.

At first they heaped reproaches upon him.

"You were a stranger, and I took you in," the Patriarch said. "I treated you as one of my own family, and this is how you repay me."

"It is not me," replied Louis, lightly. "Could I have brought you away and left the rest unharmed I would have done so; but the Tourgovons were resolved upon killing their foes.

"They were our foes," said Felix. "We were never theirs."

"I know nothing about it," said Louis, "save that they made the demand. It was their price for services rendered to me, and I had to pay it."

He was in a bantering vein, and, with the pride and fortitude of Spartans, they braced themself to treat him with contempt.

Clara did not speak or even look at him, and two or three remarks he made to her were uttered to the deafest ears—those wilfully deaf.

The spot chosen by Louis for his new home was a delightful retreat, such as Oberon and Titania and their attendant fairies would have loved.

It was one of those places to which Dame Nature does a bit in the way of embellishment.

It lay between the hills, and was about ten acres in

extent. The ground was carpeted with flowers; wild fruit abounded at the base of the hills.

There was water, and fruit. and food sufficient for the wants of primitive man.

The band had been busy erecting huts, and to one of the largest the unhappy captives were conducted as the dawn was breaking.

It was divided into three compartments, all at present in an unfinished state.

'By-and-bye," said Louis, " I hope to make you more comfortable. Believe me, I am not the true author of your misfortunes."

"Say no more," interrupted Felix. "I would rather talk with a devil than with a hypocrite."

"Well, you will know me better by-and-bye," answered Louis, unruffled.

Left to themselves, the captives gave way to grief; but the men had no tears.

It was Clara who wept, and it was well she did so, for it relieved her.

Anon they talked of the possibility of an escape.

Intuitively they all understood why they had been brought thither. The looks in the manner of Louis when speaking to Clara conveyed the story of his most unholy love.

An hour later one of the men brought them breakfast.

He scowled at them as he placed it on the ground, and uttered a few taunting words.

Felix, whose arms, as well as the arms of his friends, had been set free, promptly knocked him down.

With a savage cry he sprang to his feet again and drew a pistol from his pocket.

Before he could use it Louis strode up and stepped between him and Felix.

"What now, you dog?" he cried.

The "dog" quailed before the eye of his leader, and, with a muttered anathema on Felix, replaced his weapon.

"Get you gone," said Louis. "I shall not forget this. Dare to exhibit your wolf's temper again and I will end it. You can guess how."

Turning to his prisoners he said—

"I regret this exceedingly. It shall not occur again. I will myself attend upon you."

They did not demur to his proposal, nor assent to it. They simply said nothing.

With all his callousness it stung him to the quick, and he stood there for a moment biting his nether lip.

"I see. You are determined to misunderstand me, he said. "Now, suppose I repay you by giving you up to these men?"

He looked at Clara as he spoke, and the shaft he shot hit home.

Her cheeks paled, and an affrighted glance from her eye was directed to Felix.

"*I am your only friend here*, said Louis, sternly. "Remember [that ! I alone stand between you and a terrible fate.

As he spoke he pulled the door to, and seemed to be going away. But the next moment he opened it again.

"If you make the least attempt to escape," he said, "I will hand you over to the tender mercies of your foes."

Then he closed the door again and sauntered away.

It was a cunning device of his to utter this threat, and he knew it would be a stronger hold than chains on the two men.

As for Clara, she would never attempt to escape alone.

Louis, though secured from any serious attack, kept his men on duty, and one was posted on an eminence to watch. Two men were also despatched to the coast to obtain some shell-fish.

It was the latter that brought Louis some strange news in the evening.

On reaching the coast they had wandered several miles northward, coming in sight at last of a dark object in the distance, which they thought was some huge animal.

Venturing nearer, they found it was the hull of a ship—a wreck, stranded on the shore.

Its masts had been sawn off short, and since its

Hal quietly awaited the onslaught of his foe.

stranding there was evidence of its having been recently despoiled of some of its contents.

They judged it had not been many days ashore.

This was startling news, for it pointed to the probability of there being a crew or some body of men on shore.

Louis could not believe it was the vessel he had not long before deserted, and the two dunderheads who brought back the report had omitted to look for the name.

Louis dispatched a man at once to find out, bidding him watch all night and return in the morning.

For once Louis was very much perturbed.

Whatever the vessel might be, it could bring him no good future, supposing the crew were safe ashore.

If an ordinary body of seamen, they would have no sympathy with him or his pursuits, and might prove troublesome.

If the men of the Diadem had reached the shore they would prove to be no less antagonistic to him.

They would realise that he had selfishly deserted them, in the full belief that they had gone down to the bottom of the sea, and would trouble him no more.

So he passed a night of doubt and of anxiety, and found what relief he could from the report of the man when he returned.

It was the Diadem, and the crew—the crew that he desired to drown—were camped in the shelter of a wood, about a mile from the shore.

"An unkind scurvy trick," said Louis, to himself, " for Fate to play me.   They outnumber us two to one. But courage ! If they do not discover us here all will be well."

CHAPTER XII.

HAL IS TAKEN PRISONER—INTERVIEW WITH HIS BROTHER—LEFT TO PERISH.

HAL and Grip were among the hills scouting for Louis and his captives. In two days they had wandered here and there, finding nothing to reward them for their pains.

But though discovering nothing themselves they did not remain undetected.

One of the scouts set by the watchful Louis perceived them, and with all speed reported their presence.

In half an hour Louis, with five of his men, were on their track.

Prior to leaving, Louis took the precaution to secure the door of the hut that held his captives, and setting a guard over it to kill either or both of the men within if they attempted to escape.

Clara, at any rate, was to be spared.

Louis, more wary and fox-like than his brother, kept well out of sight after he had discovered Hal.

Like a sleuth-hound he tracked him to a spot where he and Grip lay down to sleep.

Then he crept up, and while they were as yet half awake secured them.

Bound like a felon, Hal was led back to the haunt of Louis, who went on before, in his eager haste to assure himself of Clara's safety.

Arriving there, Hal and his faithful servitor were separated, and the former was guarded all night by two men, who never ceased to pass up and down before him.

Early in the morning Louis, with two others of his band, appeared, and now indeed a full recognition took place.

Hal had not much of his old fire in him.

Two weary days of marching, with little food, followed by a sleepless night, had left him little strength, but he was neither broken nor subdued.

"A strange meeting, brother mine?" said Louis.

"A bitter meeting," answered Hal; "and yet I have prayed that we might never meet again."

"A brotherly petition, truly."

"I have dreamt of you, Louis, and although I am not given to superstitions I have been forewarned of evil to follow between us. Enough, the prophecy is fulfilled."

He bent his head for a moment, and so pale and wan did he look that Louis signalled to one of his men to take off his bonds.

Seating himself on a big stone, Louis looked at him

coolly and critically.

"Hal," he said, "you are not wearing well; a life of travel and excitement does not suit you."

"Do not mock me," said Hal, with a forward angry gesture, which was checked by one of the men grasping his arm.

"I am in no mocking mood," returned Louis, "but in deadly earnest. Now, Hal, it would ill become me to take your life, for you are my brother."

"Take it," said Hal, bitterly; "it is barely worth my keeping."

"Gently," replied Louis; "anon, if necessary. Now listen, Hal. With all your hatred of me—"

"Louis!"

"Your hatred of me, I say, although you do not care to show it, you are one whom I can trust if you give your word. You must go from here and never return."

"Louis," said Hal, "I am seeking friends, and ere I go I must find them."

"Your friends are safe," sneered Louis; "you must trust them to my keeping. The gentle Clara and I are already fast friends."

"Louis, you are lying," cried Hal.

"Ah! that was spoken like you," answered Louis. "I would take your word, and I expect you to accept mine."

"If you have one grain of the true man in you," cried Hal, "do not hurt Clara."

"Of course not," said Louis. "I will be as gentle to her as lover can be. Ah! you may start, Hal, and frown, but I have as much right to love her as you have."

"Love!" said Hal; "*your* love?"

"Well, it is acceptable to her," said Louis, "and there is an end to that. The father lives, the brother lives, and we shall all ere long be settled down into a family party. Now, Hal, be reasonable, and do nothing to spoil it."

"I cannot bear this," said Hal. "Louis, I will not go.'

"You must," was the cool reply.

"I will not, though it costs me my life—my love—"

"*Your* love?"

"Yes; we are affianced, and love and duty bids me stay. Louis, in all your graceless life you have never done so cruel an act as you now contemplate. Do not go beyond the talking of it. Make it an idle threat."

"What, give her to you, Hal?"

"No; not unless you permit it. You say you will take my word. Release her and her father and brother. Let us go at once and seek some place of safety, and I swear to you that as soon as it is found I will leave here for ever."

Louis laughed.

His brother's promise tickled him as an excellent joke might have done.

"You mean it, Hal, *now*," he said, "but when once away—safe out of my clutches—and she reminds you of your vows, what will you do? May you not make a sacrifice for her sake, and break your word?"

"I swear I will not, Louis."

"No, my good fellow, I cannot trust you, as you are only mortal. Now, Hal, give me your word that, if I release you, you will depart and trouble me no more, and you are free?"

"And if I refuse?"

"You will have twenty-four hours to change your mind, and if unchanged by that time you will be shot—you and that quixotic old fool, Grip, together."

"I will not go," Hal said.

"Enough!" returned Louis. "Bind him again and guard him until the morrow."

But Hal had suddenly broken away. With one blow he laid the nearest ruffian on the ground, and a second blow sent another staggering back.

Then, as the others presented their weapons at him, he turned and fled.

"Fire! Kill him!" hissed Louis, as he sprang to his feet.

Both men fired, but Hal escaped unharmed, and bounded on—up the rugged side of the hill.

Suddenly one of the scouts rose up from behind a rock and sought to bar his way.

Hal closed with him and a struggle began.

A fierce fight for the possession of the scout's weapon followed, and Hal's foot slipping, he and the scout rolled down the hill in company.

All too quickly the others were upon him, and Hal fought for life and liberty, while his brother looked calmly on.

How could an exhausted man hold out against so many?

They secured him again, and bound, and almost breathless, he stood before his brother.

"Louis," said Hal, "from this hour I cast off the tie of blood between us. You and I are no longer brothers, but mortal foes. I will treat you as I would any other man who has done me a cruelty and injustice."

"Bravely spoken!" laughed Louis; "but I fear you will have little chance to exercise your hatred. Lead him back, and shut him up somewhere alone. I hold you responsible for his appearance when I shall need him."

Hal again resisted, but with little effect.

They dragged him back to the village, and threw him into one of their huts.

It was, although but recently built, anything but an agreeable abode for Hal. The odour of ruffianism was in it.

Having got him there, they secured his legs, in addition to his arms, and left him helpless.

In a little while they brought Grip there too. He was also bound hand and foot, and, as they threw him on the ground upon his face, so he had to lie until he could, by slow, laborious effort, turn himself over.

"Oh! Master Hal," he said, "this is a terrible pass for you to come to."

"For both," replied Hal, gloomily. "Oh! may the day swiftly pass, and to-morrow come."

"We'll be hopeful yet, Master Hal."

"Hopeful of what? Mercy from my brother Louis?"

"No, Master Hal—I'm not so mad as to dream of that —but hopeful of getting free ourselves. There are many hours between now and daylight to-morrow."

"Ah! Grip, you were ever cheery. But think of *her* —of Clara—a prisoner in HIS hands. We cannot hope to escape, or save her."

"I'll not give up hope," said Grip, doggedly, "until I feel the bullet in my heart, and then I shall have no time to say much about it. Can you get a little nearer to me?"

"There is only a foot between us."

"But you must come nearer. Those cords of yours can be bitten through, and I have good teeth."

"So have I," replied Hal. "Let me start on yours."

"No, I will begin, Master Hal; and as I'm bent on it don't waste any time talking about it."

Hal saw that he was determined and yielded.

By a slow process he worked himself nearer to Grip, and then turned over upon his side.

"We must not be discovered at this work, Grip," he said.

"No," was the answer. "You keep quiet while I'm a doing it. Not a sound, and all our four ears open."

Hal turned over, and Grip began upon the knots that had been tied in the rope between the arms and behind his back.

It was a hard, greasy rope, and would have required a stout knife to cut it. Strong as Grip's teeth were they could only slowly bite through strand after strand.

After a few minutes he rested, panting from his labours.

"It is the unkindest rope I ever tackled," he said.

"While you rest, Grip," replied Hal, "let me have a turn at yours."

"No," returned Grip; "not with those delicate white teeth of yours. When I have got through your rope, and you are free, you can find some other way of breaking my bonds."

Hal yielded, and in a few moments Grip was at work again.

For an hour he worked and rested, and there was one strand severed.

But there were many more.

It was a closely twisted rope, and he saw that he could not rest this side of midnight if he wished to complete his work.

"I'm getting on, Master Hal," he said, hopefully.

He was about to renew his labours when the door of the hut suddenly opened, and one of the men entered.

He was the chosen lieutenant of Louis—a man called Cavanet. He was half Russian and half French, and possessed all the bad qualities of both nations without any of their good ones.

"Ah! my friends," he said, "how close you keep together. This is too chummy-like, as you English say. Come, we must separate you a little."

As he spoke he took Grip by the back and dragged him half-way across the hut.

He was about to bestow a similar attention on Hal, but changed his mind.

"If you move again," he said, "I will have you separated. There is no need for you to be so near each other. How do I know what fiends' plot you are hatching to escape?"

Both the listeners' hearts leaped into their mouths They thought he had been watching them.

But it was not so.

He spoke in jest, believing in his heart that escape was impossible.

"Now mind this," he said, "the next time I find you close together I will separate you; and remember this, I am only just outside and may pop in at any minute."

So saying he went out and closed the door.

There was a long silence in the wretched hut after he had gone. Hal was the first to break it.

"Grip," he said, "you have laboured in vain."

"At present," replied Grip, "but it's only during the daylight. When night comes we shall have nearly twelve hours' darkness. Then I can work."

For the present it seemed that they could do nothing but lie still, and both soon relapsed into silence.

Leaving them there, we will see what Louis is doing.

Ready-witted enough to turn everything to account, he had visited his other captives and told them of his having secured his brother Hal, and he intimated that his life and liberty depended on his friends.

"If it depends on us," said the patriarch, "he is free."

"Old man," said Louis, "there is Hal's gaoler," pointing at Clara. "I will be frank with you. Let her consent to be my wife and the life of my brother shall be spared. If she refuses—he dies."

The old man favoured him with a long, steady look, so full of unutterable horror that even Louis could not stand it. He shrank back a little.

Felix's face was burning with indignation.

"So that is your offer?" he said. "Is Hal aware of it?'

"He is ; and begs her to save him."

"Clara, what think you of that ?"

"It is a lie," she said, as quietly and incisively as the thrust of a very sharp knife.

Few men can stand being told to their face that they lie. The cheeks of Louis flushed.

"It is a rough way of expressing your doubt," he said.

"Possibly," replied Clara. "If Hal would accept his liberty on those terms he is not the man I loved. But you lie. I can see it—your cheeks—and eyes—your air is that of one who tells a brazen falsehood !"

"I cannot talk with such people," said Louis, and with a mock courtly bow he left them.

Oh ! how wearily the day passed, but it came to an end at last.

All through the sunlit hours Hal and Grip had not ventured to make an effort to approach each other.

No food nor water had been brought them, and Cavanat returned no more.

It is needless to say that they suffered terribly both from hunger and thirst.

The latter was to them, as with similar sufferers, the harder to bear.

They bore it stoically, and as soon as the hut was wrapped in darkness Grip and Hal began to move towards each other.

Bound hand and foot, they could only move a straw's-breadth at a time, and it seemed to them as if hours had elapsed ere they were in touch of each other.

But at last Hal's foot touched Grip's head.

In the dark they had failed to keep quite the correct course, and now an upward movement on the part of Grip was necessary.

It was soon carried through, and then over again Grip began his strange and heart-breaking labour, nibbling with his teeth as the mouse does in the fable at the meshes that held the lion captive.

CHAPTER XIII.

THE VISIT TO THE HUT—RESCUE—THE HIDING-PLACE IN THE MOUNTAINS.

GRIP, having got into position, renewed his efforts to bite through the rope, but, alas! he speedily found the task too much for him.

His earlier efforts, followed by additional captivity, had worn him out.

After a few attempts to bite the rope he sank back with a groan.

"You cannot do it, Grip," said Hal.

"I'll try again in a minute," replied Grip.

"You shall do nothing of the sort. Come, Grip, it is my turn to try with you."

"Hush!" said Grip.

The door of the hut was softly opening.

As it hung on leathern hinges only it did not creak; but Grip had suddenly caught a glimpse of a strip of sky, and guessed that somebody was entering the hut.

They both lay quite still, hardly daring to breathe.

Whoever it was, they did not intend to make any noise.

Softly he came in, and the door was closed.

"Anyone here?" he asked, quietly.

"You know we are here," replied Hal. "Why try jests or tricks upon us?"

"Who are you?" asked the intruder.

"Hal Warrington and his friend Grip," was the reply.

"Ah! I know that voice," said the other. "Do you

not know mine ?"

"I fancy I have heard it before," said Hal.

"Call to mind the morning when a mad fool, at the bidding of a villain, sought to run his lance through you. He failed, and you spared his life."

"I remember. And you—"

"Are the man you spared—Adrian Tourgovon."

"Have you come to help me ?" asked Hal, wonderingly.

"No ; I did not know you were here. I came to save others, but I can help you too.

As he spoke he advanced cautiously until his feet touched those of Grip.

Then he knelt down.

"You are bound," he said, "by the Tourgovon's knot. There is no need to cut it ; it can be easily loosened if you know the way."

As he spoke Grip felt his bonds suddenly relax, and then with an effort he got his arms free.

Sitting up, he rubbed his half-numbed limbs, and soon began to experience the tortures of reaction.

But he cared not for that.

He was free !

"Master Hal," he said, softly, "where are you ?"

"Here, released from my bonds," replied Hal, joyfully.

"Hush !" said Adrian Tourgovon ; "not so loud. Softly ! They may hear you, although they do not keep a very close watch."

"You say you do not come to save me," softly asked Hal. "Whom did you come to save ?"

"The Menlonvitches—father, son, and daughter," replied Adrian.

"I thought you were their enemy ?"

"I was," said Adrian, between his teeth, "but now I will be their friend, if only to thwart that villain who has usurped me in the leading of my people !"

"Let that be our united task," said Hal.

"Nay, mine alone," returned Adrian. "I have freed you. Do not rob me of the good such a deed may do."

"Where are they ?"

"That I do not quite know; captive in one of the huts. I thought they were here, having watched earlier in the day, and seen Cavanat go in and out."

"But cannot I help you?"

"No; one may creep about in safety, two will lead to discovery."

"I suppose I must yield," said Hal, reluctantly. "What are we to do?"

"Remain here until I return," said Adrian. "If I do come back I shall bring tidings of their safety."

To persist in going against the wishes of his deliverer might imperil the safety of all, so Hal yielded, and gave his word that he would remain until Adrian returned, or until lengthened absence would speak of failure.

So Adrian stole out again as he had come in, noiseless as a shadow, and Hal and Grip nerved themselves for a long and anxious wait.

Neither were in the mood for talking, but stood quite still by the door, listening for any sounds that might arise.

But all was still.

There was no sound, not even the ordinary noises of the night, in the little valley.

Hal opened the door an inch or so and peeped out.

The heavens were full of stars, but the valley was wrapped in gloom.

Not a sound.

Not a whisper.

Opening the door a little further Hal tried to pierce the gloom, and soon his eyes began to put a shape to the ill-defined things around him.

He could make out the outline of a hut on the right, then that of another or the left, and, finally, he thought he saw moving figures away in front.

He could not tell whether they were of man or woman, and while he watched they melted away.

"Has he succeeded?" was the question Hal asked himself.

It was a momentous thought, and the answer soon came.

In the gloom ahead a single form shaped itself and grew in density as it approached, until it was near enough for Hal to make out that it was Adrian.

Then he drew back.

The Russian came up to the door, and softly said—

" Are you there ?"

" Yes," was the answer.

" Take off your boots and follow me."

Quickly their boots were removed, and they glided out.

Not a word was said as they crossed the camping-ground of Louis Warrington and his followers, not until they were ascending the hill beyond, when Adrian halted.

" The way is very rough now," he said ; " we may resume our boots "

He had his own slung around his neck, and, sitting down, he proceeded to put them on.

To be able to do so likewise was very grateful to Hal and Grip, for the road was rough everywhere, and had sorely tried their feet.

" Where are our friends ?" Hal now ventured to ask.

" I have sent them on," replied Adrian. " They ought to know their way. I trust they will not make any mistake."

" It is possible for them to do so ?"

" Yes."

" Then I would rather have been left to my fate than risk her life."

" You speak of the beautiful Clara ?" said Adrian, rather bitterly. " But it is nothing to me. She will never love me. What care I, so long as I keep her from that villain ?"

He led the way up by what looked like a road, although dimly seen, until he came to a rock that stood up like a pillar.

This he left on the right, and took a downward course.

" We return to almost the level of the plain," he said. " It is a good hiding-place."

The path was now nothing but a simple descent from one broken rock to another until they came to level ground again.   Pointing ahead, Adrian said—

"Yonder is a wall of rock that will hide us from our foes.   See ! there are our friends.   Ha ! only two.   Where is the third ?"

He ran forward, followed by Hal, and in a few moments Hal was beside Clara.   The other one was Felix.

" Hal !"

" Clara !"

A few words of hurried explanation were exchanged, and it was known to Hal that the patriarch had somehow strayed from his children.

" We were cautious'y feeling our way, and were near be bottom," said Felix, " when we missed him.   He must have strayed out of the path."·

" If so," said Adrian, " I can find him.   Come here with me.   Let me put you in a place of safety.   I discovered it one day when out hunting, and never told my friends of it.   I rejoice now that I could keep a secret."

In the more open space where they were there was less gloom, and a waning moon was coming to their assistance.

Adrian's hiding-place was a cavity formed by an avalanche of rocks that had fallen down the mountain-side in some remote age—the result, no doubt, of earthquakes.

The entrance was narrow, but inside there was plenty of room, and as the light grew stronger it crept through the crevices and openings, revealing a strange natural temple, divided by barriers of stone into several chambers.

Hal did not, however, linger then to examine it.

Having seen Clara into a place of safety, he started off with Adrian to find the patriarch.

As soon as they were well away Adrian said—

" It will be useless to look for him."

" Why ?" asked Hal.

" He has probably fallen over some small precipice, and is dead.   There are a hundred such around us."

" Living or dead," said Hal, " we must find him."

" It is a useless search," returned Adrian.

It occurred to Hal that Adrian was not eager for the work before him, and he offered to do it alone

His offer was accepted with some eagerness.

"I am too tired," said the Russian; "but do not go very far, so that you cannot retrace your steps when daylight comes."

So saying he turned away and hastened back to the lower ground.

Hal kept to the course they had used for the descent, and whenever he came to anything that looked like a precipice he went to the edge and peered over.

For the most part they were mere hollows, and the depths were easily penetrated. Others were dark and deep, and if anything had been lying below it would hardly have been distinguished by the keenest eyesight.

Hal reached the conical rock where the road turned downwards, and took a seat upon a stone.

The night was almost over, and daylight would soon be here.

Weary with fatigue and excitement he felt he must rest awhile ere he could go on, and while resting he slept.

Sleep did not come upon him as it does in the ordinary way, but suddenly, as if an extinguisher had been put over him mentally and physically.

From a dense dreamless sleep he aroused by the warm rays of the sun upon his face.

Awaking he found that great luminary two hours high, and with a feeling of reproach he leaped to his feet.

Looking around he could see the spot where his friends were in hiding, but none were visible to him.

Turning his gaze to the other side he beheld a sight that astounded him.

The huts recently occupied by Louis Warrington and his men were all ablaze, and the occupants had disappeared.

Nor was this all.

Away yet farther and clear of the hill he saw a figure.

Once seen it was not likely to be forgotten

It was the old patriarch.

He was fleeing before two men who carried rifles in their hands.

These men were strangers to Hal. As far as he knew

he had never seen them before.

He did not recognise in those two any member of the Tourgovon family.

How the old man had got there was, of course, a mystery; but to speculate on such a matter would have been a waste of time.

The patriarch was flying away from Hal. He and the men also had their backs to our hero.

Refreshed by sleep, he boldly dashed down the mountain side, leaping from craig to craig with an agility and sureness of foot that rivalled the mountain goat.

Unharmed and saved from so much as a single fall by what must be looked upon as a series of miracles he reached the plain and started off in pursuit.

The patriarch was running at a pace wonderful in one of his years; but the men were gaining on him.

Hal could hear them calling on him to stop.

Their voices were English.

The speed they ran was nothing very great, and Hal gained upon them.

As he drew near he could hear the pursuers cursing the old man and vowing they would shoot him if he did not pull up.

He did not answer them then or so much as look back.

On he went, with his pursuers after him.

And Hal gained upon them unheard, and, therefore, unheeded.

"I can't go much further," he heard one of the men gasp.

"Shoot him!" cried the other.

They were within a few yards of the patriarch, but it was clear they were dead beat, and had either to shoot him down or let him go.

They stopped and levelled their rifles.

Then Hal dashed in front, turned, and seizing the barrels of the weapons pushed them up.

"Would you shoot an old man, you cowards?" he cried.

The old man heard him, stopped, and turned.

"It is my English friend!" he cried. "Oh! marvel-ious."

And exhausted he sank to the ground.

CHAPTER XIV.

THE ITALIAN'S STORY—THE BOAT UPON THE SHORE—FLIGHT.

THE two men having relaxed their hold on the guns, drew back, staring at Hal.

The suddenness of his appearance and the promptness of his action took them completely by surprise.

Dropping one of the guns, and putting his foot upon it, Hal presented the other at them, and bade them stand.

They looked at each other as if in doubt what to do, and then yielded.

"Who are you?" Hal asked.

"We are Italians, signor," one of them answered. "Until lately we served in a ship which was lost. It sprung a leak and sunk at sea."

"By what right do you attack a defenceless old man?" demanded Hal.

"It was a jest and no more," replied one of them, with a laugh. "We were driving him to our camp in the wood yonder."

"You would not have harmed him?"

"No, signor. On meeting us he fled, and we gave chase. It was but fun—you call it fun—we did it."

They were rough-looking fellows, but with a humorous expression of face that softened down their apparent ruffianism.

"How many are there of you?" asked Hal.

"Six of us," was the answer, "and fully a score of our children."

"What do you mean?"

"Behold!" said the Italian. "We were at sea—our ship leaked—she sank—we take to our boats six strong, the rest go down. It is so. We row, row, until our arms ache—land at last, and the hull of a drifting ship with men on board. The ship is sinking, they cry for help. We row—we row, and tow that ship—oh! so slowly—we

D

beach her.   Then they tell me her story."

The fellow was very dramatic, and Hal was interested.
Possibly the story of that ship might concern him in some
way.

"The ship was doomed; a knave of knaves first lead
the men on to mutiny, then make them drunk, then drills
holes in the hold and flies, leaving them to die.   But it
was not to be.   They escape—they camp in the woods—
they see a man prowling near the hill upon the shore—
they follow him home, and behold him—the traitor is
there.   Last night they attack him—he flies, leaving dead
behind him.   They burn his huts, and he is an outcast.
It was just."

It was bitter for Hal to hear of further infamy on the
part of his brother, but he was growing used to it.   His
heart was fast hardening against him.

"Your story may be true," he said, "but the fact remains: I caught you in the act of slaying my friend—you
forfeit your arms. Take your lives, and return to your friends."

"For a moment a scowl rested on their faces; then
they looked at each other and smiled.

"He says it is to be so—let it be so," said the one
who had not spoken.

"Yes," said the other.   "Signor, farewell!   We may
meet again.   Until then, adios!"

They kissed their finger-tips, and strode away with the
gait of muscular dancing-masters.

Hal turned to the father of the Menlonvitches, and
said—

"You are anxiously waited for.   Are you strong
enough to accompany me?"

"I think so," replied the patriarch; "but I am somewhat sore.   I slipped and fell when following my son and
daughter; the shock rendered me insensible, and when
I recovered I was too confused to clearly know my way.
I wandered here and there until the morning was no
longer young.   When I fell in with you Italian thieves,
I was weak, unstrung, and fled.   You know the rest."

Hal took him by the arm, and led him back.

As they were reascending the hill, they saw Felix and

Adrian approaching.

Felix came bounding down to his father's aide, and fell upon his neck weeping with joy.

When this demonstration was over they hastened on, and were soon all beneath the shelter provided by Adrian Tourgovon.

But there they could not stay for ever.

The country around them was alive with foes. They must get away.

But whither could they go?

A few words in the story told by the Italians had given Hal a clue.

They came thither in a boat, and it must be somewhere on the shore.

The direction was clearly indicated by the road the Italians had taken.

If they could gain possession of that boat they could put to sea, and make their way along the coast to a more frequented part of the wide waters.

Hal put his scheme before them, and they all agreed that it would be a great and grand thing for them to obtain possession of that boat.

"Here," said Felix, "we have foes on every side. I would rather trust to the tender mercies of the sharks of the ocean than to them. To-night I will seek and find that boat."

They all rested during the day, sleeping in snatches, save Adrian, who stole out and brought them in some fruit and roots for food.

Poor fare, but better than nothing.

And when night came they all started to go with Felix. As soon as the sun set they begun their stealthy march, walking quietly and not speaking for fear of foes.

Down to the sea they wended their way, and walked along the shore, until they came to the hull of the Diadem lying on its beam ends.

On the other side of it was the boat they sought, square set and strongly built. The very thing for a sea journey.

Quietly they launched her, and when nearly afloat, Clara and her father were desired to get into it.

When they had done so the rest pushed off, and Grip and Adrian took their seats, each with a long sweep-like oar.

Barely had they settled down when a voice was heard from the shore—

"What ho ! boat there."

"Don't answer," said Grip, with set teeth : "pull."

"Boat there !" cried the voice again. "Is that you, Ponto? Speak out, or I fire !"

"Crouch down," whispered Hal to Clara.

She obeyed, and the next moment the report of a rifl was heard.

A bullet went singing over their heads to sea.

Then a shouting was heard inland, and the man on the beach answered back.

Our friends in the boat heard the dull thud of feet hurrying over the sand, and then there was more shouting for them to return.

"Lie close," said Hal to Clara.

The report of firearms was heard again, and bullets went past, whistling on either side of them. The aim of the man on shore was wild and hurried.

Grip and Adrian strained every nerve at their oars. Hal but steered.

All the others bowed their heads, so as to give as little mark for the men on shore to aim at.

Slowly and steadly they pulled out to sea, and all things on shore faded out of sight.

"The tide is with us," said Adrian ; "it is going out."

It was so.

The wind, likewise, was in their favour, and they were carried out to sea beyond the reach of danger.

CHAPTER XV.

ADRIFT ON THE SEA—A TIME OF SUFFERING—IN A NEW LAND—A BIT OF A SHOCK.

THE night grew dark, and black clouds, which had, in Hal's experience, been rare in that region, came up from the horizon and obscured the stars.

The waves, at first insignificant swellings, increased in size, and the boat got some rough tossing, which would have tried one of less substantial structure.

Adrian and Felix had some little experience of the sea, but not much. The others had none to speak of.

Hal soon perceived that their position was a somewhat perilous one for every now and then the boat in the darkness would be caught almost broadside on by a wave.

Adrian had now taken the helm, and Hal sat by his side ready to give a hand in case of emergency.

They were all silent, each occupied with his own thoughts.

The morning came—not cold as we have it here, but warm, and with a mist upon the sea.

Half an hour after the sun was up that mist was gone, and they found themselves out of sight of land.

This was not in accordance with their arrangements, and they were too far from the old shore to attempt to run back against the strong wind that was blowing.

But without food or water the outlook was not cheering.

But there was no signs of dismay on the faces of any of them.

" We had better go on," they all said ; " perhaps we may fall in with some vessel."

They thought it probable—or said as much ; but the day passed and no craft of any description came in sight.

A hot sun brought on thirst, but none complained.

Hunger, a lesser evil, but trying to hale, hearty men, assailed them.

Then evening came, and far away ahead of them a line of cloud-like appearance rose up in the horizon.

But they soon lost it in the gloom of night.

" Perhaps it is a coming storm," they said, "and it will bring us rain."

They thought less of the perils of a storm than of the pangs of thirst.

But there was no storm.

The stars came out and the wind fell almost to nothing. Taking their turn at the oars—all save the patriarch—they doggedly rowed on.

It was about midnight, and Hal and Grip were rowing, when Adrian, who was steering, said, grimly—

"The clouds are nearing us now; we shall soon have rain."

But as he spoke the boat suddenly grounded in soft sand, and threw the occupants of the boat together.

"Land !" they cried, joyfully.

The cloud which they had seen was land, and now, in the dim starlight, they could make out the outline of cliffs and hills, or mountains it might be, rising high in the air.

Hal leaped out, and the other men followed, and together they drew the boat up high and dry clear of the gentle rollers that just lapped the shore.

It was enough for all there—it was land; and all their thoughts turned to one thing—water.

Hal, with Clara leaning on his arm, followed the men, who walked at first slowly and painfully after being so many hours confined to a sitting position.

The noise of a cascade soon drew them to it, and the all-consuming pangs of thirst were dispelled.

Hunger they could endure, and, wearied out, they stretched themselves in the cool, soft sand and slept.

Morning again, and the glories of a new land to gladden their eyes.

Or if not a new land it was far away from the spot where they had previously dwelt.

It was a rugged, picturesque coast, offering nothing to eat but the shell-fish on the shore. Life on the coast would hardly be endurable.

Altogether, although saved from immediate starvation, the prospect was not entirely cloudless.

None of them knew where they were.

If on an island, they could not be any very great distance from the mainland. It was necessary they should obtain some definite information on this head.

Grip and Hal volunteered for this service, as being the two best fitted for it.

The air was soft and warm; it was like an opiate, and they both fell asleep while on their journey.

They were, like the lotus-eaters the poets sing of, lulled into a dreamy, sensuous state that was like the opium-eater's false paradise.

As they lay there a wild-looking savage came sauntering along.

His dark body was ornamented with wooden beads and feathers, and his head was crowned with a heavy crop of coarse black hair.

He carried a spear in his hand, twirling it in a jaunty manner as if he had no need to fear a foe.

Suddenly he caught sight of the two sleeping men.

It was such a shock to him that he fairly bounded back and stood with his big dark eyes standing out of his head.

After a long stare he wheeled round and bounded off like a startled antelope.

The dreamers slept on.

Half an hour elapsed without their being disturbed, and then the savage appeared again.

He was creeping on his hands and knees, and close behind him came a second native.

Further on there was a third and a fourth.

As stealthily as cats the foremost two men crept up and stared first at Hal and then at his gun, which was lying by his side.

CHAPTER XVI.

TERAPAI, KING OF THE VOLU-VOLUS—THE IRON SERPENT—HONOUR TO THE MIGHTY.

IT was evident, from their pantomimic actions and wild staring that a white man and his weapon were alike novel to them.

One of them took up the gun and looked at it.

He stroked the shining barrel and carefully felt the stock.

The others came up, and they all got upon their feet.

So intent were they upon examining the rifle that for a time they all seemed to forget the sleepers.

The savage who held the weapon began to finger the lock.

One of the others took hold of the barrel and looked down it. He made most strenuous endeavours to see what was inside.

Then he put a finger inside and felt carefully about, but with no better success.

After that he put his eye to it again.

They were all silent, wrapped in wonderment.

Another savage took his turn at the barrel, and was just in the act of putting his eye up to it when—Bang!

The gentleman who had been persistently manipulating the trigger suddenly brought it down and fired the weapon.

The effect of the explosion upon them was amazing.

They turned back head over heels, then got up and fled for their lives.

Save and except the gentleman who had taken his turn at the barrel.

He lay on his back, with head as bald as he was born with, and his arms and legs spread-eagled like some warrior lying dead upon the battle-field.

A mile or so away, surrounded by a multitude of followers, King Terapai, head of the Volu-Volu people, sat upon his throne.

It was a barbarously built throne of wood, ornamented with tiger skins and rudely made ornaments of gold. Terapai was a gigantic savage, much feathered and painted.

He was not an idle monarch, but a brawny athlete who had made his voice heard and arm felt in wars with rival tribes; but he was, in common with his swarthy brethren, much given to superstitious rites and observances.

He had many medicine men among his people, the chief of whom was Ranu-few, who now stood beside his king in the proud position of his general friend and adviser.

Terapai was meditating an onslaught upon a rival, but prior to entering upon that sacred duty of slaying and robbing his neighbour, he wished to know if all things were propitious.

Ranu-few was going to see.

The people had assembled, and Ranu-few was about to begin, when there burst into the throng three terrified savages, who immediately threw themselves full length before the king, which is the polite way of the tribe of asking for permission to speak.

We give, in a translated form, the conversation which ensued.

"What ails my slaves?" said the king.

"Oh! Terapai, biggest king of the earth," cried the foremost, "we have seen and heard wonders"

"Is there a greater wonder than I am?" asked Terapai. "Speak!"

"Oh! king, we have seen two men," cried the foremost, "with no colour in their faces. They slept, and by the side of each was a straight, stiff serpent, which belched out fire and spoke thunder."

The king was startled.

Ranu-few and all the people around shivered.

Ranu-few kept calm.

He was so perpetually practising gammon that he was prepared to hear of any and every sort of gammon from others.

"The serpent spoke," continued the speaker; "and lo! Wabla's head blazed. He fell—and died."

But Wabla was not dead.

He heard the account of his demise as he came striding through the throng with his head as bald as an egg and singed like a goose for the cooking.

To add to his charms, his eyes were well out of his head, and his lips quivered.

"Who is this?" demanded the king.

"It is Wabla!" shrieked the front trio.

And all the people cried—

"Wabla—Wabla! But, see! the serpent hath burned his hair."

There was no getting over this bit of evidence of the power of the fiery serpent, and Ranu-few looked a bit non-plussed.

But he still kept fairly calm.

The king looked at him.

"What says Ranu-few?" he asked.

"The god of the Volu Volus will eat the stiff thunder serpent," replied Ranu-few, who naturally had his doubts about the story.

He thought that Wabla had somehow set his head on fire, and as the loss of hair was a serious thing for a Volu-Volu, robbing him of all dignity, had got up a yarn to account for his loss.

"Where are these men without colour?" asked Terapai.

His informants pointed in the direction they had come.

"Let us go to them," said the king.

He rose up, and Ranu-few, having picked up the god and tucked it under his arm, took a place at the king's side.

The informants were told to go on, and Wabla of the Burnt Head, as he was called, was put into the post of honour in the van.

Now Hal and Grip, who were aroused from their slumbers, had seen Wabla, of the Burnt Head, come out of his trance and bound away at a pace that made pursuit quite hopeless.

They let him go, and Hal, having loaded his gun again, said—

"We have not landed in a deserted island."

"Maybe, he's the only one," replied Grip, "he seems to have given himself a scare."

Little dreaming of Terapai and his host they went forward on their way, both suffering from a peculiar languor, which they put down to the relaxing air.

Suddenly two great bodies of savages were seen sweeping round the wood.

The demeanour of the savages was very friendly.

Terapai stuck his spear point downwards into the ground and threw up his arms as a sign that he meant peace.

Hal and Grip turned their rifles downward and advanced.

Signs of amity were exchanged, and step by step the king and the strangers drew nearer to each other.

Terapai pointed at Grip's rifle, and in his native tongue asked for it to "speak."

Hal could not understand the language; but he got at the idea from the signs made by the king.

He was helped to this conclusion by Wabla, who was commanded to come forward and exhibit the ludicrous state of his poll.

He also had another man brought forward and expressed a desire to have *his* HAIR removed in the same way.

Hal had some difficulty in keeping his countenance, and Grip's face was warped with a grim smile.

But Hal could not risk doing by design what had been done by accident, so he comprised the matter by taking up a large stone and throwing it into the air.

As it descended he fired at it, shattering the stone to pieces.

Then Terapai leaped into the air, and all his people fell flat upon the ground.

Ranu-few was shaken to his very centre by fear; but all that made life dear to him was at stake, and he smiled a smile which said—

"That is nothing. It is a mean trick which any fool could do."

But he was not prepared for the action of Terapai, who turned to him and said—

"Speak like the stiff serpent—roar. Throw up a stone and break it.

To which Ranu-few replied—

"Another day—oh! king. I must get in more wind. I am not ready."

"Ask your god to make you ready," said Terapai.

"He, too, must have time," replied Rana-few.

"Then he is no god," said Terapai. "Bear him away to the big water and drown him."

Hal and Grip stood quietly by, wondering what was being said. It was not at all clear to them at first.

Ranu-few was petrified.

Drown the god! What profanity—what sacrilege!

Of course, he did not use those words, but something

equivalent to them in his native tongue.

He would not do it himself—he dare not, and he defied any member of the tribe to do it.

Terapai smiled scornfully.

"It is no god," he said. "It cannot walk or speak; it cannot speak in a whisper, and the stiff serpent can roar like thunder. That shall be the god of my people."

Then without any more ado he raised his leg and made a football of the god.

He kicked it up about twenty feet into the air, making it spin like a tip-cat.

It descended with a rush, fell upon its head, and lay most ignominiously on its back.

Then ensued a scene of wild commotion.

Ranu-few struck a defiant attitude before Terapai, and the king rushed for his spear.

He would have skewered the medicine man if he had not fled, calling on all the tribe to follow him.

He picked up the god on his way, and, holding it aloft, dashed away to the wood.

Some of the people, about a third of the tribe, followed him.

The rest stood steadfast by their king, being no doubt induced to do so by the fears engendered within them by the "stiff serpent."

Dark grew the brow of Terapai.

In his anger he looked like what he was—a magnificent specimen of savage life.

He shook his fist in the direction of those who had deserted him, and then, turning to Hal, threw himself upon the ground and embraced his feet.

CHAPTER XVII.

WELL CARED-FOR CAPTIVES — THE REBELLION OF RANU-FEW—CROSSING THE FORD.

HAL was now in a very embarrassing position.

The whole of the remaining part of the tribe surrounded him and Grip and began to sing a song of praise, and

Terapai, having risen from the ground, embraced him like a brother.

After that Grip was, much to his disgust, favoured with a hug, and he was asked to make his "stiff serpent" speak.

"Master Hal," he said, "I calls this a reglar waste of good ammunition, and we haven't much to spare."

"Never mind," said Hal, "fire away. It will keep us friends with this brawny fellow; we shall be able to slip away by-and-bye."

Grip fired his rifle, to the great terror and excitement of the natives, and was rewarded with another embrace.

Then the king wanted to hear both weapons speak together, but that with barrels unloaded could not be done.

Hal made signs to the effect that the "stiff serpents" did not like to talk too much, but might do so again by-and-bye.

He did not care to let the king into the mystery of loading them, which might go far to rob the weapons of their power over him.

Terapai looked a bit downcast, but he soon recovered and motioned for the tribe to march.

He led the way, with Hal and Grip on either side of him, and the people behind in sixes, marching in good order.

They were certainly well disciplined.

"Master Hal," said Grip, "where is he going to?"

"We must go with him," replied Hal.

Terapai listened intently. He endeavoured to learn their tongue.

"Go!" he said, pointing ahead.

It was a marvellously quick catching of a word and its meaning. Hal saw that he and the swarthy king would soon be able to converse—that is, if they kept long in each other's company.

On they went.

And during a short halt, Hal and Grip began to stroll away in the most casual manner.

But the king was instantly after them.

He did not seem to doubt them, but he certainly did not mean to let them go.

With two such medicine-men he felt himself the most powerful king on earth.

They marched on about two miles, and then entered a wood, in the centre of which stood a huge stone building, which looked as if it had been standing a thousand years at least.

It came upon Hal as a complete surprise, but Terapia was familiar with it.

It was his home.

Who had fashioned it he had no conception, and possibly believed it had been made by the hands of some god.

It was at least seventy feet high, very solid in front, and surmounted by a sloping roof. A flight of steps led up to an open door.

Up these steps Terapai led his captive medicine-men, ushering them into a vast hall lighted by holes made in the roof by time and decay.

It was sombre and oppressive, but it had one quality especially desirable in that climate—it was cool.

And that, no doubt, was the reason why Terapai had chosen it for a home.

It was large enough to hold some hundreds of people, but only a chosen few followed the king into its friendly shelter.

The rest squatted on the flight of steps and the ground outside.

For three days were Hal and Grip captives there.

They were allowed to roam at times, but always with a friendly escort that could not be shaken off.

And they were not allowed to go very far.

If they showed a tendency to get away from the temple they were always gently warned to go back.

And back they had to go, for there was no knowing how the king might take any act of disobedience.

On their anxiety about their friends we need not dwell.

It may be guessed at by anyone who for a moment will place himself in their position.

On the morning of the fourth day Hal was aroused by a yelling and stamping, mingled with a clashing of spears outside.

He sprang to his feet, and found that he and Grip were the sole occupants of the huge hall.

They ran to the doorway, and looked out upon a scene the like of which they had never beheld before.

Ranu-few, with his rebel friends, had attacked Terapai's men while they slept.

That is, the men made the attack, while Ranu-few stood in the rear, with his squint-eyed god raised in the air, where he was now yelling and capering.

Our friends did not, however, stay to survey the scene.

"Grip," said Hal, "It is now or, perhaps, never."

They walked to the edge of the top of the flight of steps, and, unperceived by Terapai and his friends, jumped down and bore away to the left.

On the bank of the river they stopped to take breath and look back.

From out of the wood a number of savages were running for their lives, and foremost came Ranu-few, with his god tucked under his arm.

There was now very urgent need for them to get across the river.

Caution was necessary, for the stones were slippery, and here and there deep pools, with eddies, were discernible.

With naked feet it would have been easy enough, but boots are not good things for travelling on a slippery road.

Like beginners on the tight-rope they began their journey, balancing themselves with great care, and their eyes fixed on the stones immediately before them.

Half-way across Hal was startled to hear a yell in front of him.

He looked up and saw a swarm of savages on the opposite bank, and some already on the slippery stones crossing over.

One, indeed, was quite near him, a wild-eyed, ferocious savage, who was surprised, but not alarmed, at the sight of him.

The savage, indeed, sprang forward and tried to seize him.

Quick as thought Hal had him by the throat, and endeavoured to throw him into the water.

The very act overbalanced him, and the two fell into a pool of water together.

Grip had been as much taken aback as Hal by the unexpected appearance of another body of foes.

CHAPTER XVIII.

A BRIEF REST AND A BARBAROUS BRUTE—RANU-FEW AND HIS FOLLOWERS GETTING READY FOR A GRAND CEREMONY.

FOR the moment Hal forgot to use his weapon, but now he pointed it at another savage who, with gleaming eyes, was making towards him.

Bang !

A thousand echoes were awakened on every side as the savage leaped up, and, turning a half-somersault, pitched head first into the seething water.

Another immediately behind him fell off in sheer fright, and the others yelled in dreadful chorus.

For an instant they remained staring at him, and then in wild disorder scattered and fled.

So far well, but the report had been heard by Tapai and his men in pursuit of Ranu-few and his rebel followers.

The king, foremost in the pursuit, turned his dark eyes in the direction of the sound, and saw Grip steadying himself after firing.

Hal and the savage were struggling in the water, keeping themselves afloat by the force of their struggles for the mastery.

The eddying water bore them to a shallower place, and they got a foothold.

Hal still held on with one hand, clinging to his rifle with the other.

It encumbered him, but its value was too great for him to cast it aside.

The huge anaconda struck out viciously.

The savage had dropped his weapon, or it would have been all up with him.

The eyes of Terapai gleamed angrily.

He saw that Grip and Hal, his two great medicine-men, were endeavouring to get away from him.

It was an unfortunate time for them to seek safety in flight, for all his savage blood was aroused by the attack made upon him by Ranu-few.

He called off his men, and dashed in pursuit of Grip and Hal.

They came bounding on like greyhounds, and Grip saw them coming.

"Master Hal," he cried, "throw off that nigger and get across!"

But the nigger was not so easily to be thrown aside.

He held on, and he tried his best to overpower Hal.

They twisted this way and that with such rapidity that Grip dare not shoot.

And Terapai was coming on with lightning speed.

"Master Hal," he cried, "the whole lot are close upon us!"

"Get across and save yourself," answered Hal. "I'll get rid of this fellow and follow."

But Grip would not desert his leader.

They had lived and travelled far together, and, if need be, he would die with the only man he cared for on earth.

Terapai was now by the river-side, brandishing his spear and uttering ear-piercing cries.

Behind him were his men, bloodthirsty and strong—their hands and bodies stained with the gore of those they had slain.

"It's all over with us," thought Grip.

It went against him to hurt Terapai, who had, after all, done them no wrong—but what else could he do?

Turning, and balancing himself on two stepping-stones, he pointed his rifle at the savage king.

"Stand back!" he cried.

Terapai understood the action, if not the words, but he did not quail.

Under his dark skin there lay as brave a heart as ever

beat in the bosom of man, white or black.

Boldly he stepped forward, and, with a quick, light step, approached the determined Grip.

Hal and his foe were still struggling for the mastery.

"I must do it," thought Grip. "It goes against the grain, but he is our foe now."

He did not mean to kill Terapai, but only to maim him, and aimed at his thigh.

"It must be done!" he gasped, and pulled the trigger.

Terapai stopped short, and clapped his hand to his leg.

Grip saw the blood spurting out, and groaned.

He felt it was almost an unworthy thing that he had done.

But Terapai did not fall.

After a moment's delay he started on again, with his eyes like balls of fire.

There was the savage lust of murder in his eyes.

He had worshipped Hal and Grip, even as he had once worshipped Ranu-few, and both had turned upon him and become foes.

He was ready like a lion to avenge his wrongs.

So on he came, and Grip was now practically unarmed.

There was no time to reload.

He turned his eyes towards Hal, and saw that it fared ill with him likewise.

He had fallen in a few inches of water, and his muscular assailant had got above him.

His naked, bony knees were on his chest, and he had a hand upon Hal's throat.

Without help the savage would choke the life out of him.

There was not a moment to be lost, and Grip, heedless of all else save the necessity of immediately giving aid to his master, went to his assistance.

From stone to stone he went quickly, and, having reached the pool, leaped into it and fought his way through it to the shallow water.

Gaining a foothold he raised his rifle, and with the butt of i: dealt the savage a blow that laid him senseless.

Then he grasped Hal's coat and raised him to his feet.

Only just in time to turn and face Terapai, who had now come up to the pool, and, spear in hand, was in the act of leaping into it.

But, as Terapai leaped down, his over-taxed energies yielded.

No doubt he had exerted himself prodigiously in the fight with Ranu-few and the rebel members of the tribe.

The loss of blood from the wound Grip was compelled to inflict brought on utter exhaustion.

And, with his fall, Grip rallied.

Endowed with new strength, he fought his way to Hal and with a blow from the butt-end of his rifle laid his antagonist low.

"Mas er Hal," cried Grip, "rouse yourself. '

Hal made an effort to do so, but he was half-dazed; and, but for the assistance of his faithful follower, would have perished there.

Grip looked around, and saw that, so far as immediate danger was concerned, they were safe.

Terapai lay senseless on a pile of broken stones, his followers had not dared to follow him, and the foe that came from the other shore had disappeared.

Hal soon recovered himself so as to be able to speak.

"Good Grip !" he said.   "I had given up all as lost ; but I might have known that you were not far off."

Instinctively he picked up his gun, and, fighting against the sense of weakness that was upon him, essayed once more to cross the river.

After some slipping and blundering, he and Grip reached the opposite side, and then, for the first time, he became aware of what had happened to Terapai.

The Volu-Volus, on the retreat of the "two white medicine men," went to the rescue of their king, whom they lifted up and bore from his precarious position to the shore.

Grip explained to Hal the circumstances that had compelled him to put that amiable monarch *hors de combat.*

"It is a pity, Grip," said Hal; "but I do not see how you could have done otherwise. But the worst of it is that we shall now have him as a foe. We must recross the river sooner or later, if we are to see our friends again."

"H'm," said Grip, "I'd overlooked that."

A great part of the morning was now spent, but there were many hours daylight for them to utilise, and having watched the last of the Volu-Volus into the wood, they began their backward journey across the stepping-stones.

Owing to their being unable to make close observation of the passing country during their march, they twice got quite out of the track, and evening had come when they arrived at the spot where the king sat down and received the intelligence of the arrival of the two white medicine-men with the stiff serpents who spoke with the voice of thunder.

Here they halted for the night, feeling it would not be safe to go further, and, having chosen a resting-place under some trees, they lay down to sleep.

It was a moonless night, but the stars shone out with tropical radiance, and objects of any size could be faintly seen some distance off.

So it happened that Hal, who lay thinking, for sleep refused to come at the wooing, saw a number of men approaching.

Having quietly awakened Grip, who was dreaming of the old life at home, he whispered a few words of caution in his ears, and they both watched the movements of the advancing men.

They approached in a manner which showed they were not searching for anyone, so Hal decided that he and Grip had no cause for fear.

He simply changed their place of retreat to one more secluded.

Ensconced behind some densely-growing bushes they waited for the strangers.

Strangers, however, they were not.

It was Ranu-few and the remnant of his followers—a sorry band of about three score.

The spot where King Terapai sat that day was the chosen one for sacrifice and conciliation of the Volu-Volu god, and Ranu-few had come thither for some oracular help to bring about confusion on the king who had given him and his rebel assistants a thorough good thrashing.

Ranu-few had his precious idol, none the better in appearance for the rough treatment it had of late received, which he placed on or near the spot where it had been on the previous occasion, as recorded.

Some of his followers then set to work to light a fire, searching for tinder wood, and producing it by friction in a sort of bowl.

Two other large bowls were there, in which was placed some of the tempting berries growing on the island.

These Ranu-few pounded, and added something he drew from a small pouch he wore, which set the whole in a ferment.

By this time the fire was blazing merrily, and by its light the two watchers could see the eager savage faces turned towards the bowl in which Ranu-few was brewing a drink which, of all devilish liquids, has rarely been equalled, and certainly never surpassed.

CHAPTER XIX.

DRINKING. "SHIMTI"—ITS MAD VOTARIES—MISSING FRIENDS—NEW FOES.

THE bowl was ready.

The fermentation was very strong while it lasted ; but it soon ceased, and Ranu-few signalled to his followers, with a cry of " Shimti," to form a circle.

They did so, throwing up their arms and uttering cries of joy.

Ranu-few threw up his right arm, and immediately there was silence.

Then he threw himself on his face before his god, and uttered a few words with great rapidity, finishing off with shrieks.

Leaping to his feet, he seized the wooden bowl of liquid and placed it to the lips of the god.

Then he put it to his own, and Hal saw that he did not drink, but only pretended to do so.

It was not so with his followers.

They drank eagerly, and had to be checked by Ranu-few, or there would not have been sufficient for the whole circle to have tasted.

They all drank in deep silence, and after the bowl had passed round, a loud, concerted shout rent the air.

Then they were silent again.

Like statues the whole circle stood, with Ranu-few beside his god, watching each face in turn.

Suddenly as if moved by some powerful outside agency, one of the first to drink leaped into the centre of the ring and began to dance.

His example was infectious.

The spirit without and the spirit within moved all the rest, one after the other, and soon all were dancing.

And such dancing !

Not the dancing of men, but of fiends.

No words could describe their wild and frenzied movements, nor pencil or brush do justice to the scene.

They twisted, twirled themselves down headlong, leapt up again, shrieked, yelled, groaned, and fought with the air, and finally began to inflict injuries on themselves that were cruel, appalling surgical operations.

And all the time Ranu-few looked on, doing nothing save watch the movements of his deluded followers.

When he thought they had gone far enough, he put his hands to his mouth and uttered a cry that could be heard a mile away, so loud and shrill was it.

This was the signal for the " festivities " to cease.

But the Volu-Volus had either been maddened or their blood was hotter than usual, for they would not stop.

On the contrary, they leaped, and turned, and yelled the more.

Ranu few picked up his god and, holding it aloft, stalked among the maddened men, crying on them to be still.

Then, governed by some hidden demon, two of the men fell upon him and cast him down.

Immediately, like a pack of wolves, the whole band were upon him.

It was a heap of struggling, yelling humanity, pulling this way, tearing that, and high above their shouts rose the screams of the tortured Ranu-few.

His followers, in their madness, were tearing him limb from limb.

Such was the effect of the vile drink upon them.

At all times too potent, but only used on rare occasions, Ranu-few had that night made it stronger than was customary, with a result terrible and fatal to himself.

The engineer was hoist with his own petard.

When all was over, when Ranu-few, by false inspiration, had brought himself to a terrible end, and the satiated murderers had stolen away, Hal rose up and turned his back upon the scene.

They rested no more that night. Neither felt it possible to do so. This dark land seemed stained with blood and was burdened with untold horrors.

They kept what they believed to be the right course; but in a strange land, with no light but the stars to guide them, it was inevitable they should lose ground.

So indeed they found in the morning, having struck the line of hills three miles or more south of the flat spot, where they descended to the plain.

That was a matter of small moment, and an hour later they were in sight of the temporary camping-ground of their friends.

There was the ground, but where were Clara, Felix, and the rest?

They had vanished with their belongings as into thin air.

There was no sign of their recent presence, and as far as the look of the place went, they might have been the creatures of a dream.

"Can this be the spot?" asked Hal, as he looked round him in amazement.

"Yes," replied Grip, "I don't see any doubt of it. That pile of stones on the rim of the cliff up yonder is the same. We can't very well be mistaken.

For in a niche they discovered a small bundle. In it

was a suit of clothes which Felix had once offered to Hal. There was also a small dagger which had been Clara's.

Were these things left for him?

It seemed so, and Hal had need of these clothes, for his own were getting worn, and had recently been torn, so he put them on.

Again and again they examined the spot, and were forced to come to the conclusion that there was no error in the matter.

But whither had their friends been wafted?

Every other vestige of their recent presence had been wiped away. It was like being in a land of enchantment, with a wicked magician working evil.

Hal had no thoughts in that direction, but he was sorely troubled. Everything conspired to make his life one of unrest.

There was the possibility of a ship having, in passing by, stopped and taken off the refugees; but surely they would not have abandoned him without leaving some sign of whither they had gone?

An hour later they were scaling a cliff with the vague hope of finding some signs of their lost friends. They were silent und weary, each busy with his thoughts. Had they been more attentive to their surroundings they might have seen that their movements were being watched by half-a-dozen men who were skulking behind the projections of the summit of the cliff.

They made no forward movement until Hal and Grip had reached the summit of the cliff, and were standing on the verge of it looking seaward.

Then they came up stealthily in the rear, and one, with the butt-end of a rifle, struck Grip down.

Hal heard the blow and faced about, received a blow himself which caused him to sink to his knee—so near the edge of the precipice that he was in imminent danger of falling over.

"Yield!" was the command in English, with a strong German accent. "We are determined to haf you—traitare! villain!"

Hal, half-stunned by the blow and deprived of the

assistance of Grip, could offer but a feeble resistance. Indeed, he would have fallen over the cliff but for the assistance of his foes, who, strange to say, did not seem eager to take his life.

The leader was the German who had spoken, and when Hal had been dragged forward and his hands bound he addressed him with much exultation.

"To come so far, and to so zoon succeed; ah! it is goot."

"What have I done to you?" demanded Hal.

"Noting," was the answer; "but to my friend—mooch."

Grip, whose hands had also been tied behind him, had now partly recovered himself, and was sitting up looking ruefully about him.

Meanwhile the half-dozen ruffians, with great coolness, quite in a business-like manner, kept watch over him.

"Master Hal," Grip cried, "what is the meaning of this?"

"I have asked this man here," replied Hal; "but he answers like a fool."

The two captives, yielding to circumstances, got upon their feet and walked away with their captors, who took a northern course away from the spot known to our friends, and at a favourable place descended to the shore where they were ordered on board a boat.

Hal and Grip were sent forward to lie down and "gif no troubles," and the whole party having embarked, two huge sails were hoisted, and the boat stood out to sea.

As there was really no danger of escaping, their hands were released, and they were allowed to sit up and look about them.

The land they left behind them became like a cloud, as we have said, and ahead another cloud rose up from the sea.

It was a thin, flat cloud, with a cone rising in the centre, so regular in shape that it was difficult to believe it to be the work of Nature; but as it did not change, Hal was satisfied that it was some mountain.

Night came, and a wretched time it was for the prisoners.

The man at the helm was changed thrice in the night, but whoever was there smoked a long cigar, of which there was a liberal supply on board, and the glow of it was in Hal's eyes a fiery star, until at last he slept.

He was awakened after a long and troubled sleep by a pressure from the hand of Grip, and, starting up, he looked around him.

CHAPTER XX.

THE LAND OF THE CONE—HERR SCHMITZE CONFIDENT —THE SLOWEST PEOPLE IN THE WORLD—OFF TC THE GREAT HERR.

NIGHT had gone and day had come again. Such peril: as they had encountered at sea were over. The lumber ing boat was close in shore, under the shadow of the grea' cone, that rose up to an enormous height and kissed the very clouds.

It was a most imposing, yet simple, scene. The vasi mountain was a perfect cone, and apparently as smooth from base to summit as a well-laid-down grass slope.

At the foot of it, near the sea, there was an assemblage of crude houses and settlers' huts, and behind these were indications of some sort of mining operations going on.

Hal took all this in at a glance, but he had no time to make any comment upon it ; for one of the crew brought forward some coarse bread and coffee, and bade him and Grip " eat him oop."

And, furthermore, he stayed to see him do it, partaking of his own breakfast at the same time.

The rest of the crew, with their self-satisfied leader, were also eating and drinking in a stolid, silent way that was very depressing.

Ashore there did not seem to be anybody stirring ; but that could be accounted for by the early hour.

Hal and Grip partook of the food given them as a necessity.

Like their captors, they were silent, and when they had finished two of the crew came forward and re-bound their arms.

"Why could not this be left undone?" asked Hal. "What crime have we committed that you should treat us as malefactors?"

"You are tiefs," was the simple response.

"Thieves!" exclaimed Hal. "And, pray, what have we stolen?"

Here the leader came forward, filling his pipe as he did so, and bade his man be silent.

"It is off me to speak," he said to Hal. "Vat you steal—mooch? When I take you to ze Great Herr you know; for now I tell you noting."

"Perhaps you have nothing to tell," suggested Grip.

The eye of the German, or whatever he was, lighted up for a moment in anger; but it died away again.

"In time, I shall haf enough to tell to—HANG YOU," he said.

There was sufficient of the startling in this announcement to make both Hal and Grip feel uncomfortable; but the former was satisfied some mistake had been made, and that matters would be explained.

Little did he think, however, how near that mistake would be brought home to him.

The men had now got the boat in close to the landing-stage, and, as they were making it secure, a heavy-eyed man came to the door of a hut close by.

He had nothing on but his trousers, shirt, and a pair of heavy boots, and sleep still hovered about him, for he yawned like a hippopotamus.

Then, resting from that form of labour, he took a look at the sea and sky, and finally saw the boat, which was within a few yards of his nose.

By a slow process, an expression of profound astonishment dawned and developed in his face.

"Schmitze!" he said, at last.

The leader of the crew replied—

"It is so. See, I haf got dem, Karl. You see 'em?"

Karl stared hard at Hal and Grip, but did not exhibit

any sign of recognition.

"Schmitze," he said, "you haf NOT got dem."

"Karl," said Schmitze, "you are a fool."

On hearing this, the whole of the crew gave vent, as one man, to a guttural—

"Zo!"

Schmitze took two or three puffs at his pipe, and stared round him, and then said—

"You are all fools!"

Karl was not offended, but had another yawn, and came into the open.

Now there was a general movement in the place, and men and women came down to the landing-stage, where they stared at the prisoners.

And Schmitze declared a dozen times, at least—

"See!—I haf ze tiefs."

To which they all responded in the same words and the precise manner as Karl—

"Schmitze, you haf NOT got dem."

For their temerity they were all called fools, and told to wait until the "Great Herr" had seen the prisoners.

Beyond the fact that Schmitze had made a mistake the stolid community did not appear to take much interest in their friends, but they exhibited a little more vitality when it was announced that "Lutz vas dead."

Lutz was the gambler who had been wounded the day before, and the unlucky fellow had died during the night, in all probability alone.

Everybody had a question to ask about him.

"How did he die—and who killed him?" or something that way; and the questions were answered to the apparent satisfaction of everybody.

One man, who was spoken of as his brother, made legal claim of all the dead man's possessions, and he gave a hand in bringing the body ashore and laying it, with some attempts at decency, on a bench outside one of the huts.

They covered the dead man's face, and his brother, pickaxe in hand, went away to dig his grave.

Hal looked on this scene with natural wonderment, marvelling at the slow-blooded way of these people, who seemed to be a mixture of the German race and others he could not even guess at.

They were slower than Germans usually are, which is saying a great deal; the ordinary Teuton is generally brisk and smart compared to these people.

Schmitze appeared to take the adverse criticisms on the prisoners much to heart.

He was one of those men who never do wrong, and cannot by any possible means make a mistake. Even when made clear to them that they have done so they blame the facts and not themselves.

He came ashore and sat down on a block of wood, with his eyes on his prisoners, while his men put everything taut on board the boat.

They were so terribly slow about it that Hal tlought they never would have done.

Every bit of rope was coiled as if it had been an enormous iron cable, and the grunting that went on during the performance was like that of a score of self-satisfied pigs in a farmyard.

But at last everything was finished and Schmitze arose.

"Ve vill now go to ze Great Herr," he said.

A hand was laid upon his shoulder, and, turning, he saw Karl.

"Vell," he said.

"Schmitze," said Karl, "you are wrong. It is not ze men."

"Karl, you are a fool!"

"It is so, Schmitze—all men are fools; but zere are wrong and right fools. You are a wrong fool."

The placidity of Karl was a delightful study, and Hal could not help laughing.

The brow of Schmitze darkened.

"When ze Great Herr see dem," he said, "he say to me—'Schmitze, you are wise—you are like oder fools;' and he reward me—"

"Wif dis," said Karl, significantly slapping his boot with his hand.

Then all the crew laughed, and every man slapped his boot as Karl had done.

Notwithstanding the serious nature of his position—and Hal knew it was serious—he laughed heartily.

Grip's hard face was broadened by a prodigious grin.

Schmitze arose.

"Bring ze prisoners—de tiefs !" he said.

But here a difficulty arose.

The crew were quite willing to accompany the prisoners ashore, but no further.

They one and all declared they would not go to the "Great Herr" with them.

"For," as one said, "ze Herr's boots are big, and he do not like to be made a fool of."

"I go alone," said Schmitze, taking up his gun, and signaling to Hal and Grip to go forward. "Turn and march."

It was humiliating; but with their arms bound they were helpless, and after an exchange of glances, expressive of their mixed feelings, they set out, bearing to the left of the great mountain.

The inhabitants generally followed them to the outskirts of the houses, chaffing Schmitze in a ponderous way; and he smoked convulsively, sending out great clouds of smoke, but saying nothing in reply.

Like many other great men who had been derided and disbelieved, he knew that his hour would come, and his calumniators and aspersers be confuted.

Outside the town, or camp, or whatever they called it, the land was smooth and covered with grass; but there was a tolerably well-defined path leading around the base of the mountain.

The most notable eature of the landscape at this spot was the entire absence of shrubs and trees, but in the distance Hal saw that this monotony was broken up.

Presently the path brought them into quite a clump of trees and bushes, in front of which was a big wooden fence, and nestling inside was a wooden house of some pretensions.

This, no doubt, was the residence of the Great Herr, and Hal ventured to ask if he had surmised aright.

"It is so," said Schmitze, complacently. "It is ze

place you rob and run away from."

Hal knew it would be useless to argue with a man of such fixed opinions, so he contented himself by saying—

"Oh ! that is the place. I did not recognise it."

"Ze Great Herr," said Schmitze, "ven he was rob say —'Bring me ze man and let me see him zat I may hang him, and ze man zat bring him here is mine friend.' "

And Schmitze smote himself on the knee in a manner that said—

"Here's the man !"

"Grip," said Hal, quietly.

"Yes, Master Hal?"

"I'm in hopes that we shall be able to put matters right with the Great Herr ; but if he should prove to be as big a fool as this fellow, we will try a run for it, and trust to what follows."

"Whatever you settle on, Master Hal," said Grip, "I'm ready for."

CHAPTER XXI.

SCHMITZE FINDS OUT WHAT HE IS—THE GREAT HERR AND HIS MINE.

As Schmitze and his prisoners drew near the gate of the house a ponderous man, smoking a big pipe, appeared in the garden.

He came slowly down to the fence, so that his arrival timed with that of Schmitze on the other side.

Hal and Grip halted a little in the rear to await developments.

If matters looked threatening Hal made up his mind to run for it ; but he was not without hope of the error, whatever it was, being cleared up by the "Great Herr."

Schmitze saluted, and drew himself up with a satisfied smile.

"Vell?" said the Great Herr.

"Look—behold !" cried Schmitze, pointing at Hal and Grip.

"I see," said the Great Herr. "Who am dey?"

"One is de big tief," replied Schmitze.

The Great Herr looked at Schmitze in a quiet, penetrating way, and then said—

"You are a great fool!"

He also added an adjective which was quite superfluous, for his manner of uttering the other words left nothing to be desired.

"A—fool!" Schmitze gasped.

"Where you git dese strangers from?" asked the Great Herr.

"From de Western Island," was the reply. "You send me to find him."

"Not him, but de great tief. Oh! Schmitze, you ARE a fool. What did dese strangers do to you?"

"Noting. I find 'em and bring him—both."

"Oh! it is a fool you are, Schmitze," said the Great Herr. "Vat do I see—you tie zere hands? Cut de cords. Oh! you fool."

Schmitze with a dazed expression of face proceeded to comply with this order. Meanwhile the Great Herr opened the gate and came slowly out.

When the ropes had been removed he held out both his hands.

"It vas wrong," he said. "But Schmitze is a fool, and I vas one to let him go in search of ze tief. Come into mine house and have meats and drinks."

Then he turned and said, in the severest manner, to the crestfallen Schmitze—

"Look ze oder vay."

Schmitze, with tears in his eyes, did so, and the Great Herr lifted his big boot with such effect that the mistaken captor was projected forward several feet.

"Go back to ze mine, you fool!" he said.

The whole thing was so astonishing to Hal that hitherto he had said nothing to the Great Herr, but now, as Schmitze was walking away with a decided limp, he proceeded to thank him for having set them free.

"Vat else could I do?" asked the Great Herr. "You must be sent back again. Come in and tell me who you are, and all about you."

The house of the Great Herr was not by any means a palace.

It was big and roomy, and it had furniture in it, but everything was the work of unpractised hands.

He conducted his guests into a room facing the way they came, and having sunk into a rough but strong chair, he bade his guests be seated also.

There was a table and a cupboard in the room, and a bedstead, but no attempt had been made to hide the rough logs put together with tolerable neatness.

The window was an open one, without glass or any substitute.

The Great Herr clapped his hands, and, after a short delay, a stout, short woman waddled into the room.

"Mine spouse," said the Great Herr.

Hal got up and bowed.

Grip touched his forelock.

The woman looked at them with a vacant, expressionless face, and said—

"Vell?"

"Somtings to eat," said the great Herr.

While she was gone to get it Hal told as much of his story as he thought necessary.

The Herr listened with great attention.

"You haf a broder whom you not agree vith?" he said.

"I do not say that," said Hal.

"No, but you say you haf one and no more. It shows there is no love."

"He and I never did agree," said Hal, lowering his head.

"And no vonder," said the great Herr. "I can understand it. But eat virst, and I vill tell you vhy."

His wife had now returned with a cloth, some bread and meat, and water.

The Herr explained they had no other drink but tea or coffee.

Hal and Grip were content with water, and while they ate he told them his story.

He was called the Great Herr because he was the

leader of a band ot adventurers who were in search ot some great mine they had heard of, hidden in the bowels of a "cone mountain," and the Herr believed they had come upon it at last.

His people were half-Germans, half-Russians, the offspring of two bands of settlers which had for many years been on the African coast, living in a hand-to-mouth sort of way, until one day a shipwrecked sailor told them of a deserted mine he had seen at the foot of a "cone mountain."

He was not quite certain of the latitude, but he gave them a fair idea of the direction to take; and the thirst for wealth broke up the settlement.

At first the people kept together, but disputes as to the way which to go led to a division in them, and the Herr became leader of those now with him.

They had found three cone mountains in all. Two were drawn blank, but the one they were now located at promised them the treasure they sought.

"Ve haf found ze mine—deserted," he said; "and ve haf found—diamonds. But ve haf zem not."

He raised his great hand, and let it fall upon the table

"Lo! It is at times ve go to oder places—for food, to hunt—what not; and one day ve find two strangers, who say zey shipwreck. I take pity on dem, bring dem here, ood—treat zem as broders, and lo! one morning zey go —take von of our boats and all mine bag of jewels, ze tiefs! Ah! you haf a broder—shall I call him Louis?"

Hal's head drooped again, but the Great Herr got up and laid a hand kindly upon his shoulder.

"Vat of zat? I had a broder—bad. He go wrong, 1 see him no more. You are not as your broder—let him go. He rob me, and, by dis pipe of mine, if I catch him —he *hang!*"

"There is one thing I should like to ask," said Hal, sadly. "Why did Schmitze seek him where he found me?"

"He vent zat way, and dere is no oder land for many miles of sea. He vent dere, and—ah! you speak of friends you lost dere. Oh! mine young friend, I am sorry for you."

Slow as he was of body, the Great Herr was not slow of brain, and into his mind there now flashed the thought that troubled Hal.

If Louis had really got to the other island might that not account for the disappearance of the patriarch, Clara, and the others?

It is true that Louis had but one comrade with him, the remnant of the band of ruffians; but he was crafty and cruel, and he might have fallen on them in the night, slain the men, and carried Clara away.

One ray of hope that it might not be so remained.

If Louis Warrington had murdered Felix and the other men, would he have taken the trouble to obliterate every sign of his crime?

Certainly it did not seem at all probable; but the depth of the mystery was still further increased.

The Herr proposed that they should stroll to the mine and see the working, and Hal gladly consented.

So they all went together, the Great Herr walking very slow and smoking very fast all the way.

As they entered the village, if the collection of huts may be called so, they saw the dejected Schmitze standing by the landing-stage, looking out to sea.

He had the look of a man with no longer any interest in the place, longing to fly away and be at rest.

About half-a-dozen more were about, gossiping in pairs, and as the Great Herr went by they bobbed and gave him "Good-day."

And the Herr responded with grave and slow courtesy by touching his cap.

The mine was just behind the village, and the entrance to it was marked by heaps of loose straw and rubbish.

It was, more correctly speaking, a tunnel, for both in the old days and now the miners worked their way into the hill.

Hal saw lights flashing in the dark interior, and it called to his mind the days when he used to read at school about Vulcan and the Cyclops, and others who laboured in the bowels of the earth.

"Enter, my friends," said the Great Herr: "and now

I tink it will be better to valk slow, as de stones and other rubbish may make you fall."

CHAPTER XXII.

WITHIN THE MINE—A GHASTLY ECHO—CLOSED UP A HUNDRED YEARS AGO—WHO WILL RE-OPEN IT?

IT was necessary that great care should be exercised, particularly at the mouth of the mine, for the ground was literally covered with rough pieces of stone of all sorts and sizes.

"Dey shall be cleared von day," said the Great Herr; "and ve vill make a proper road."

This set Hal wondering when they would begin it, and how long they would be making it, and that line of thought brought a smile to his face.

Grip's face was also troubled with a spasm which was originated by a sense of the humorous idea of these men making a road.

The entrance to the mine was about twelve feet high, and the width fully double. Inside the cave-like place expanded.

In response to a cry from the Great Herr, one of the men came towards them, bearing a light.

It was a rude kind of lantern, with a cup in it filled with tallow.   The wick was simply a piece of small-sized rope.

"Vat you all at ze end for?" asked Herr.

"Wilhelm has found an echo, Herr," was the answer.

"Is it for the first time?" asked the Herr.   "Doth not every stroke of the pick bring forth an echo here?"

"Aye, but then—it is an INSIDE echo," said the man; "come and hear."

The mine, as far as Hal could see, penetrated about seventy yards into the bowels of the mountain. It continued to expand about half that distance, and then was almost as regular in form as an ordinary tunnel.

At the bottom the miners, numbering about thirty, had assembled in a body, and there were about half-a-score lanterns throwing a fitful, dreamy light around.

On a heap of rubbish, recently dislodged by a pick, stood a tall, powerful man, with the tool in his hand.

This was the miner who had found the "inside echo."

"Here is the Herr," cried a dozen voices.

"Vat is it, my children?" asked the Herr.

"Hear!" cried Wilhelm.

All the men stood as still as mice, and Wilhelm, with his pick, struck a broad slab of stone imbedded in the wall of earth and rubbish before him.

Then came the answering echo.

It was the most extraordinary and awe-inspiring sound Hal had ever heard, so deep as to be like the growl of some mighty monster being smothered.

It lasted for fully half a minute, and then died away.

The miners were terrified, and their faces looked white in the light of the lanterns. The Great Herr was himself deeply impressed.

"Ze mountain is HOLLOW," he said.

"Perhaps it is the home of a gnome-king," suggested Wilhelm, in a voice very little above a whisper.

"Ah! it may be zo," softly chorused the miners.

The Great Herr did not deny the impossibility of it.

Like most of the northern race he was very superstitious.

Hal took a more rational view of the matter.

"There is a cavity beyond, and one of considerable extent, that is certain," he said; "but I do not think that it follows the whole mountain is hollow. May I look at the stone?"

"Look—do vat you vill," said the Great Herr, "except break your way through AT PRESENT."

Hal advanced, and Wilhelm yielded up his pick to him.

He was about to strike, when something in the appearance of the stone arrested his attention.

"This slab has been placed here," he said.

"So! By ze gnome?" said Wilhelm.

"No," returned Hal; "by the hand of man. It is only about five feet square, and is, I fancy, of no great thickness."

As he spoke he struck it with the pick harder than Wilhelm had done, and the slab immediately exhibited a crack from top to bottom.

"Hold! Vat would you do?" cried the Great Herr.

"It is done so far," replied Hal, with a smile; "but I did not intend to split it. Shall I go on?"

"My children," cried the Great Herr, "let us get into de sunlight and talk dis matter ober."

They all consented with alacrity, being awe-stricken, first by Wilhelm's discovery, and then by Hal's splitting the stone.

So in a body with unwonted alacrity they adjourned to the open, and Hal and Grip of necessity went with them.

One lantern was left burning, and the others were blown out, for it was necessary to husband their lighting power.

Then in solemn conclave they gathered about the mouth of the mine.

Ere long the women and children came, too; so also did the sorrowing Schmitze to listen, and as the discovery was deliberately discussed they gave vent to grunts of surprise, and rolled their eyes in a manner expressive of the deep emotions roused by the story they heard.

Then came the question—"Was the slab to be broken through, so that they might see what was beyond?"

"It might be done," said the Great Herr; "but who is to do it?"

Plainly none of his men; they looked aghast at the idea.

Then Hal, after exchanging a glance with Grip, said—

"I will do it."

"You?" said the Great Herr.

"Yes. Why not?"

There were murmurs of "The gnome-king!" but Hal only smiled.

"I do not fear any gnomes," he said, after a pause; "and, believe me, I think that there is behind that slab something worth discovering. My trusty friend here," extending his hand towards Grip, "and I will see what is to be seen."

"It should not be so," said Wilhelm. "Suppose dere are monsters in dere. If you break de slab you will let dem loose upon us."

"They must be poor monsters," said Hal, "if they could not break that slab without assistance. Come, my friends, there is nothing to fear; and if there is I take the risk. Grip, what say you?"

"Where you go," said Grip, "it naturally follows, Master Hal, that I go too."

"And we cannot go too soon," said Hal.

The admiration of the community was unbounded, but they were not ready to assent to the undertaking.

That idea of Wilhelm's took hold.

There might be monstrosities behind that slab, which, if let loose, would devour them all.

Dragons, huge serpents, and many other monsters connected with fairy-tales cropped up before their mental vision.

Oh! it was a great risk to run.

Still, if something were not done the mine must be abandoned, and all their dreams of wealth come to naught, for with uncertainty as to what might be hiding behind that stone, no man could work at peace.

It was the women who at last settled the question.

"As he is so brave, and is ready to risk his life," they said, "why should we be afraid to lose ours?"

"It is good," said the Great Herr; "my two brave friends shall go on the morrow."

Hal wanted to go that day—at once.

His curiosity was aroused, and he wanted to learn what secret was held by the bowels of that mountain.

He also had his dream of what might be hidden there, and he asked to be allowed to enter upon his task at once.

But the Great Herr and his followers would not hear of it.

"Ve must have time to say good-bye," they said; "it is of no hurry. Ze mountain vill not run away."

"But the monsters may break through," suggested

Hal, quietly.

"Oh! yes, it will be all ze same," said the Great Herr.

They were not to be baulked of certain ceremonies to be gone through prior to Hal's starting on his dangerous undertaking, and the first part was an adjournment to their leader's house, there to have an evening pic-nic in the garden, each contributing something towards the gastronomical feast.

It was a great and solemn feast, very plain, of course, but plenty of it. Salt fish was the staple dish, and the quantity the Russo-Germans put away was astounding.

Hal was not sorry when it was over, and he and Grip were permitted to retire to rest.

The Great Herr gave up to Hal a room which was plainly his own, and would take no denial.

"You vill vant good sleep," he said, "and it may be for ze last time."

"I hope not," said Hal, cheerily, as they shook hands and parted for the night.

In the morning Hal was stirring early, but the Great Herr and his spouse were before him.

The latter was putting up a bag of provisions of such magnitude that it brought a smile to Hal's lips.

But he did not demur to the size of it, and thanked her heartily.

They all breakfasted together—Hal, Grip, and the host and hostess.

Before the meal was over a dozen of the men appeared at the gate to act as an escort of honour to the two daring adventurers.

The party set out, and were received by the rest of the community in the village.

Hearty good wishes were expressed, and the women breathed prayers for their safety.

Hal thanked them one and all, and then, with Grip, entered the mine.

They carried each a pick and a lantern, one of the latter only being lighted, and in addition they had their bag of food and a leathern bottle filled with water.

None of the community ventured into the mine with them.

"In an hour, Grip," said Hal, "we shall know if there is anything worth discovery."

"Unless we are eaten up by those underground animals they've been talking about," said Grip, grimly.

"I do not fear them," returned Hal.

On reaching the bottom of the mine Hal bade Grip take charge of both lanterns, and hold the lighted one aloft.

Then, casting a look backwards, he saw that two or three of the more daring of the miners were peering into the cave.

He could discern that their faces were white with the apprehension that lay in their hearts.

He smote the slab with the pick-axe, and starred it all over.

The faces disappeared from the mouth of the cave.

Another blow and a portion of the slab bent inwards. A third and it fell, shattered, in a heap of fragments.

Immediately there was a rush of air that was irresistible in its force, and Grip and Hal were carried backwards, both eventually falling.

The lighted lantern was extinguished, and they were in almost complete darkness.

"What's wrong?" gasped Grip. "Is it the underground animals, or gnome-spirits, or what? Master Hal—are you all right?"

And Hal made no reply.

CHAPTER XXIII.

THE MINE EXPLODED — THE RELEASE — AN EARTHQUAKE — MARVELLOUS ESCAPE.

"MASTER HAL!" cried Grip again.

"Here," replied a faint voice. "Don't be alarmed, Grip. I was right in the full blast, and in falling struck my head against a stone."

The rush of air had now sensibly subsided, although a strong current was still coming out of the mine through the opening made by Hal.

Grip made an effort to get upon his feet, and found he had not escaped without a shaking.

A few feet away he could dimly see Hal sitting up and holding his head with his hand.

"You are badly hurt, Master Hal?" he said.

"No," Hal answered. "I got a stiffish knock, and the result is a bump on the side of my head. The skin is not broken. Where's the lantern?"

"Here."

"We must get out of the current and try to light it again. I don't see any of our friends."

"No, indeed! The first rush of air which sent forth a sound like that of a huge trumpet, had sent the settlers away, running for their lives, and they were now standing afar off, awaiting with trembling the coming forth of the monsters from the bowels of the mountain.

Hal had brought some matches with him, and by getting close up to the end of the cave, out of the powerful draught, he succeeded in relighting it.

"Take it, Grip," he said, "and keep close behind me. I shall then get as much light as I want, and perhaps it will escape being blown out again."

They cautiously passed through the opening, Hal still carrying his pick in case it should be wanted.

Once inside they found the current of air decrease in force, for the passage widened out, and also rose up higher every step.

Suddenly, not twenty steps from where they started they found themselves in what appeared to be a large cavern.

It was impossible by the light of the lantern alone to make out the dimensions of it, but the first word Hal spoke raised a rippling echo that died away somewhere in the distance.

"Grip!" he began.

Then awoke the echo—

"Grip—rip—ip—ip—p—p—p!"

They were both startled, for although not very loud it was very clear, and it sounded as if some demon was mocking him.

Grip was not quite free from superstition, and remembering all that the miners had talked about gnome kings and sprites, and what not, it is no wonder that he felt his hair rising.

"Master Hal," he said, in the softest of whispers, "it's horrible."

"It is nothing but an echo," said Hal, in the same tone; "there is nothing to be alarmed at."

But even their whispers found an echo, and it sounded very uncanny.

Hal moved on slowly and cautiously.

Grip, hugging the lantern to his breast, followed.

Keeping as straight as possible, Hal went on, counting his paces as he took them.

When he had reached a hundred he suddenly stopped.

"Bring the light here, Grip!" he said.

Forgetting the wonderful echo, he spoke aloud, and his words rolled around them like the patter of a kettle-drum.

They stood quite still until it had ceased, then Hal, taking Grip's arm, pointed towards a rent in the floor close to his feet.

It was about three feet wide, but the depth was not clear.

As far as they could see by the light of the lantern, it ran a long way, right and left.

"We can jump this," said Hal. "I will go over first, and you can throw me the lantern."

Now, short as the distance was, it was not a pleasant jump; for the bare possibility of slipping and falling into that dreadful chasm was enough to make one limp.

Hal shut his eyes—or, rather, his mind—to such a possibility, and leapt nimbly over.

"Now, the lantern, Grip," he said.

Grip carefully tossed it over, and Hal caught it.

"Hold it up, Master Hal," he said; "I ain't no hand at jumping."

Hal perfectly understood his feelings; but he said nothing.

Even a word of encouragement might have been out of place at that moment.

Grip took a short run and jumped.

But at the moment of jumping he lost his nerve, and fell short.

Happily he did not plunge down the chasm, but dropped upon his stomach on the opposite ledge.

Left to himself, he would have slipped down ; but Hal was watching for any possible mishap, and, seizing him by the coat, dragged him out of immediate danger.

"What a coward I am !" he gasped.

"Not at all," replied Hal. "I only just got over, I can tell you."

"Well, I don't think I shall ever get back again," said Grip. "It's as like pitch as can be down there."

Hal picked up a loose stone from the ground, and cast it down the chasm.

It went rumbling away down to some unknown depths, the sound of falling softening and finishing off with an unmistakable splash.

"Water !" exclaimed Hal, "and most likely an underground river."

"A what, sir ?" said Grip.

"A river down in the earth. Oh ! there are many. Philosophers teach us that there are more rivers underground than above it."

They spoke very low, and Hal, holding the lantern aloft, moved slowly forward.

A score more paces brought them to a blank wall of rock.

"Well, Grip," said Hal, "we might as well have stopped on the other side."

It really seemed so ; but, after a search up and down, Hal found a rent in the wall about six feet wide.

Lowering the lantern, he saw that the floor was not only smooth, but actually had pavement laid by human hands.

There were no possible means of doubting it ; for the stones were diamond-shaped, with a polished or very hard surface, and fitted to a nicety.

Hal now felt certain that he was on the high road to some great discovery.

On entering the chasm, he found he could converse with Grip without being bothered with those trouble-some echoes.

It was quite a relief.

"Now, Grip," he said, "our quest will soon be over. There won't be many miles of pavement of this sort."

Hal spoke jestingly, and Grip said, in a quiet way, that a dozen yards were enough for him.

The way was longer than Hal thought or hoped for, and after fifty yards or so the road branched in three directions

The difficulty now was to know which to take.

"Let us try the left first," he said, and into that passage they plunged.

The lantern gave a poor light, but their eyes were used to the gloom, and it sufficed.

Ere long the paving ceased, and the way was very rugged, the flooring being mainly masses of broken rock, which had been dislodged by the usual process of mining.

This was not encouraging, but Hal made up his mind to keep on, which showed his wisdom, for he was on the right track.

The tunnel wound about a great deal, as it often does in mines, where they follow a metal lode, and after awhile it abruptly came to an end.

Apparently there was only a rugged wall before them, but Hal continued to make his search thorough, and with the aid of a lantern, discovered another slab let into the wall.

It was smoother than the first, being at the side two feet square.

Without any hesitation Hal beat it in with his pick, and discovered a niche about three feet deep.

There were three leather bags, closely tied with some strips of the same material.

Each bag was about the size of an ordinary cocoa-nut.

Hal, with trembling hands, grasped one and gave it a squeeze.

Inside were a number of small stones that shifted as he pressed.

"Grip," he said, "we've found it."

"I'm glad of that," replied Grip; "but I don't know exactly what it is."

Hal threw open the lantern, and sitting down, untied one of the bags. He took out a handful of clear stones, which even to his unpractised eye, were uncut diamonds.

"Grip," he said, as he retied the bag, "we need not stay here another moment. We must get back again."

"And jump that chasm again?" said Grip, with a shudder.

"I am afraid," said Hal, grimly, "that it must be done."

"I'll try," said Grip, quietly; "and you must go first, as you did before."

"When you jump," said Hal, "think of one of the ditches of the old country."

"If I can I will," said Grip; "but it is fearful to think of such a place."

As they started to turn back, a rumbling was heard from the direction of the big cave, and the ground trembled under their feet.

It was followed by falling of stones from the same direction.

"Hurry up!" cried Hal. "We must not stop here."

"What was it?" gasped Grip. "One of them gnome chaps, or what?"

"It was something worse than a gnome king," said Hal. "Keep your head cool, old friend. It was the first shock of an earthquake."

As he spoke a very curious sensation was felt by both.

It was as if the whole mountain slowly rose up a short distance, and then subsided again.

They fell against each other, and the fear that they both for a moment felt was what the strongest-nerved man would have experienced.

Recovering himself a little, Hal motioned to Grip to follow him, and hastened on.

Nothing more was felt for a few moments; but Hal

knew by reading, if not by experience, that an earthquake was really an earth-wave, and one receding shock at least was inevitable.

Would there be time to get to the big cave and across those dreadful chasms before it came?

He hoped so; but, alas! his hopes were speedily dashed to the ground.

On reaching the point where the three ways diverged, he found that the shock had shaken down some of the roof of the mainway.

It was completely stopped up — they were fairly blocked in.

It was so unexpected, so horrible, that at first Hal could only stand and stare at the impassable obstacle.

Then, yielding to a momentary despair, he sat down upon the slope of the stone heap and covered his face with his hands.

"Master Hal," said Grip, in tremulous tones. "Don't give way. We can go to work and clear this rubbish away. Give me the pick."

"Useless labour," replied Hal, springing to his feet. "It would take us DAYS, Grip, to do it. We must try one of these other passages. Who knows but one or both of them may lead to the open air?"

"I'm guided by you, Master Hal," Grip said.

"We will try the centre one," Hal said.

He had the fear in his heart that neither offered an opening for escape; but anything was better than inaction.

If they were really doomed to die like rats stopped up in a hole, then it were better to seek exhaustion in movement, and so hasten the end.

As they started again there was another of those fearful upheavals, accompanied by a suppressed hissing sound.

It seemed to Hal as if the roof of the passage in which they stood was twisted this and that way, as if made of some flexible material.

But this, no doubt, was the effect of imagination.

Beyond the falling of a few pieces of stone from the sides and roof no harm ensued, and he plunged into the opening on the right, holding the lantern aloft, as before.

Under the influence of the lotus fruit.

The floor they trod on now was simply beaten earth, without pavement. It was smooth, and enabled them to get along at a great rate.

It twisted and turned about, so that at last they had no idea which way they were travelling, whether towards the original entrance or from it.

Two or three more shocks were felt, but the worst of the earthquake seemed over, and they began to gain confidence.

After awhile, exhausted with emotion and exertion, Hal was obliged to stop for rest.

Grip took advantage of the pause to trim the wick of the lantern, and on examining the fat left for burning, he reckoned it would be exhausted in half an hour.

It was true they had the other lantern, but the very thought that their means of light was so limited appalled them.

It is not strange that fear will seize upon men at such time.

Let the readers picture to themselves the awful position of these two men, shut up in the interior of a huge mountain, and, to their thinking, a very poor prospect of finding their way out again.

"When that light goes out," said Hal, "we must grope our way in the darkness for awhile. The wall is a sure guide."

Grip had no objection. If Hal had preferred they should sit down and wait for somebody to come to them, he would have assented.

"We had better eat something," was another suggestion of Hal's, and Grip again assented, although he had no appetite whatever.

But when they began to eat a strange hunger took possession of both.

They ate and ate until more than half their provisions were gone, and then they were not satisfied.

"What has come to us?" said Grip.

In a certain condition of the nervous system this desire to eat inordinately is very common. An unappeasable appetite is created by an unusual condition of the system.

This was not known to either of the adventurers, but they regarded it as something strange, and stopped eating.

"I wonder if the Herr's wife knew we should be troubled with the appetite of a wolf?" said Hal; "it looks as if she had the gift of foresight."

"It don't matter how it was," said Grip, as he put away the remainder in the bag; "it is a good thing she thought of it at all."

Once more they resumed their way along the dreadful mountainous passage. The existence of such a place was almost unaccountable, but Hal judged that the original miners, whoever they were, had followed a vein of soft soil in their working.

But it was a matter of speculation, and whether he was right or wrong he never knew.

At last the light suddenly went out, and both stopped short.

For a moment it seemed as if they were in utter darkness, and then Hal saw the faintest of faint lights ahead.

"Give me your hand, Grip," he said.

Grip's sight was not so good, and he saw nothing but darkness for some moments. Then, as the light grew stronger, but it was still very faint, he saw it.

"Daylight, Master Hal!" he cried.

"Hush! Grip," said Hal; "it seems almost too good to be true. We have not travelled far enough to have got THROUGH the mountain, and there was only one entrance on the side we know of."

"What can it be?"

"I hardly know what to think. Let us see."

They went on warily enough, and after a brief time of anxiety, came unexpectedly upon an open cave.

It was dark enough in itself, but on the left was an opening, through which came the faint stream of light they had observed.

Neither spoke, for both feared it was a delusion. Side by side they crept towards it, testing every footstep.

The opening was reached.

It was wide, but appeared to narrow lower down, and there was, without doubt, moderate daylight beyond.

"Saved !" cried Hal.

And as he spoke, the word was taken up by a hundred echoes, that rattled around them.

The truth burst upon Hal.

"Grip !" he cried, "we have wound our way back to our starting-point."

"And the big rent ?" gasped Grip.

"Oh ! that we have worked round within the solid rock—by a way probably made to avoid that hideous chasm. Never mind how we got here. We are here. Hurrah ! for life and liberty !"

With hurried footsteps they traversed the passage, reached the miners' outer cave, and found therein signs of the earthquake's working.

The floor was strewn with masses of rock shaken from the roof, and the entrance was partly blocked up. But the means of exit were ample, and with joyous cries they dashed into the open air.

CHAPTER XXIV.

THE GREAT ERUPTION AND THE TERRIFIED MINERS— A DAY AND NIGHT OF HORROR—DEPARTURE FOR THE MAINLAND.

HAL and Grip stood looking in amazement, for great changes had been wrought during their absence of some two or three hours.

All the houses or huts were lying in ruins on the ground, the boat was gone, the pier was washed away.

Above all, the great cone was split up in a dozen places near the summit, and from the crown there rose up a tall column of smoke, huge and black, rising to a great height, and then spreading out like an enormous umbrella —a hideous, awful sight for the eye of man to behold.

Over the top of the cone the lava was bubbling like broth from a huge saucepan, and in an even stream came flowing down, spreading out as it came.

From the fissues in the mountain there occasionally issued puffs of smoke and steam.

It was a terrible and fiery scene, and Hal felt thankful

that while in the mine he had no vision of its full terrors.

If he had conceived it the horror of the vision would have driven him mad, of that he was sure.

As for Grip, he was not so sensitive in a way, but dumb horror at first laid hold of him, and he could only stand and stare at the belching smoke like a man in a dream.

That the eruption should take place on the very day Hal penetrated into the mountain and found out the secret of its wealth might have had some effect upon a superstitious mind, but not upon him.

Hal saw nothing in it out of the course of nature. It was simply a coincidence.

The great thing that troubled him was the apparent act that he and Grip had been left on the island without any means of getting away from it, and should the eruption continue, the destructive fires of the volcano might overwhelm the island and compass his intentions.

It was not a pleasant look out from any point of view.

To stay where they were was dangerous, and he proposed they should go in the direction of the home of the Great Herr, with the hope of finding provisions to sustain them for a time.

He was pretty well sure it was levelled to the ground, like the miners' houses, but as he and Grip drew near it they were agreeably surprised to perceive that up to the present it had not suffered.

It stood, to all appearances, intact, being probably away from the action of the "earth wave."

Nor was this the only surprise in store for them, for on entering the garden they heard voices on the left, and turning in that direction came upon the Great Herr, his wife, and about half of the little community.

The reappearance of Hal and Grip had a startling effect upon these simple people.

They had given them up for lost, and were indeed at that moment bewailing their being buried in the bosom of the "angry mountain."

Being very superstitious, they thought the gnome king was executing his wrath upon those who had dared to invade his domain. But the return of the hardy adventurers put these ideas to flight.

The Great Herr was the first to recover his surprise, and he came forward, holding out both his hands.

"Oh! my young, brave friend," he said, "it is good to zee you."

Then they all gathered about the adventurers and plied them with a hundred questions; but Hal pleaded fatigue and postponed his narrative.

Grip, never very talkative, followed suit.

Then food and drink was given them, and while they partook of it the Herr told them what his people had done in their terror.

Hal, meanwhile, kept those wonderful bags concealed from view, and made no reference to them whatever.

After Hal and Grip had broken into the secret places in the mountain the rush of air which came forth "like a roaring beast" terrified the miners and their families, and they fled in every direction.

But on its subsiding they gathered again round the mouth of the mine and remained there until the first shock of earthquake was felt.

That they ought to have understood, for they had experienced such a thing before, although not in that island; but they cried out that the gnome king was crying out in his wrath, and some of their number rushed for the boat and tried to put to sea.

Their movements were, of course, brisker than usual, but the Herr was quicker, and, jumping into the boat, he soundly belaboured them all round and drove them out again.

Then came the splitting up of the mountain top and the belching out of fire and smoke, and the Great Herr saw that the place was no longer a home for them.

He also believed that Hal and Grip had paid the price of their temerity and perished in the mine.

A hasty consultation was held, and it was resolved that the island should be at once abandoned.

But the boat could not take more than half, and lots were drawn for those who were to go first.

Order prevailed, the lucky ones were selected, and Schmitze being one of them he took charge of the boat, which put at once to sea.

He was entrusted to take those with him to the country where he had found Hal, and to return for the rest with two men, who would be sufficient help to sail the boat.

"And I tell him," said the Herr, complacently, "that if he not come soon ZAT I COME OBER DERÆ AND KICK HIM!"

This, in the eyes of some people, may appear to be rather a wild threat, but as the Herr spoke of it with the utmost gravity Hal forbore to smile.

"Herr," he said, "I have a story to tell which I think had better be for your ear alone."

"Ve vill talk of it by-and-bye," said Herr.

Evening was drawing in and the great cone still sent out fire and smoke and occasionally shot up stones, but the violence of the eruption did not increase.

On the contrary, it was the opinion of the calmer minds that it was diminishing.

Darkness came, and as the sun went down there was a slight shock of earthquake, and the mountain for a few minutes shot out volleys of stones that rose in the air and afterwards came rolling down the mountain side.

The darkness was not darkness that night; for the fires on the mountain-top cast a lurid, weird light on land and sea.

Sleep was denied to them, save in snatches, and nobody ventured to stay long in the house.

As the hours passed, Hal, who watched the eruption intently, was satisfied that its force was diminishing.

When daylight came he was certain of it.

The column of cloud was not more than half the size it was the day before, and an upper current of air was driving the smoke away from the house and neighbourhood of the Great Herr.

He and Hal walked down to the sea, and looked in the direction the boat had taken, but there was not so much as a speck on the ocean.

Then Hal told the story of his great discovery, and frankly stared his intention of sharing his wealth with his friends.

"But I think it had better be kept a secret from them at present," he said. "Men go mad at times, when there is treasure to be had by robbing a fellow-creature or killing him; for men are only mortal, Herr."

"You speaks like a wise man," said the Herr. "Ze secret shall be kept; but for ze shares—no. I vill take as moosh as I vas robbed of—no more; ze rest is yours."

And to this point he kept.

It was, after all, the desire of a just man, and Hal was led to see it in the right light.

He had discovered the precious stones, and, but or his daring, they would have remained for ever hidden from man.

On examining the bags, the Herr declared that they were at least a hundred years old, and that the mystery of their being hidden in such a place would ever remain a mystery he was sure.

The question as to his share was soon settled.

"Give me von bag," he said. "It is more zan is my due, and enough to keep my people if ever zey get to a civilised land, and enough for me."

So it was settled.

And, with the mutual understanding to keep the great find a secret for the present, they returned to the people.

Hal had previously enjoined Grip to be silent, and, as far as he was concerned, the secret was safe.

That evening the eruption ceased, and a wonderful calm rested on land and sea.

The tired miners, who had been down to the village during the day, and dug out some of the bedding and other things from the fallen huts, camped in the open.

The Great Herr, his wife, and Hal and Grip slept in the house.

There was no haze in the morning, and again they looked out for the boat, but nothing was seen of it.

"I shall have to go and kick him," said the Great Herr.

Nothing was seen of the boat that day—nor the next—nor the next.

Provisions were running short, and the Herr was getting very angry indeed.

"Oh! zat Schmitze," he said, "he haf deserted us. Vat a kick he shall have—ven I get him."

Ah! that was just the pinch—when he got him.

Meanwhile there was a very fair prospect of those left on the island being speedily reduced to the last extremity, for it was remembered when too late that all the fishing lines and nets by means of which they used to get fish had been taken away in that boat.

Schmitze, the fool, was master of the position.

He need not return unless he pleased, and one thought haunted Hal.

Had he deserted them by way of avenging the kick the Herr gave him a few days before?

CHAPTER XXV.

AT THE LAST MOMENT—A NEW LAND—THE TRACK OF CIVILISED MEN—THE LAST STRAW.

MATTERS had got pretty well to the worst, and five days had elapsed when, late in the afternoon, Grip, who was walking by the sea looking after shell-fish, espied a sail far away to the south.

From its form he had little doubt that it was the boat returning, and he soon spread the good news among the little community.

They all came down to the beach, and were of the same opinion as Grip.

It was the boat returning.

"Zat Schmitze vill not have any kick after all," said the Herr, complacently.

There was a favouring breeze, and before sunset the boat with Schmitze and his men on board had dropped her anchor within a few yards of the shore.

As she drew little water she was able to come close in,

and Schmitze waded to land.

He was hailed with every demonstration of joy, and the Great Herr, in the presence of his people, solemnly embraced him once, twice, thrice.

On being asked why he had been so long, Schmitze explained that a contrary wind and strong currents had carried the boat past the island on to what he believed to be the mainland.

It was a rich country, and tracks of civilised people had been discovered, among other things the hoof-marks of a horse and a small piece of a bridle.

This was good news indeed, and Schmitze was embraced again by the Great Herr, as if he had been responsible for the creation of the mainland, with civilised people on it.

No time was lost in embarking the people.

Although there would be very little room to spare, the boat would hold them all.

There were five women and nine children, to whom were apportioned the cabin and the aft part of the boat.

The men, during the day and a-half which Schmitze said would be the length of their voyage, would occupy the forward part of the little craft.

With great gallantry the men carried the women through the shallow water, and one of the sights Hal remembered for many days was that of the Great Herr staggering through the water with his substantial wife upon his back.

All got safely on board with the few scraps of provision emaining.

Schmitze had brought some fruit and shell-fish ; but as a caterer he did not exhibit any remarkable talent.

All that night they sailed by the aid of the stars ; but ere they had got out of the sight of the island the cone mountain again broke out and cast the lurid light of volcanic fires across the sea.

It served Schmitze as an infallible guide, by which he could steer ; and the currents being in his favour, with a wind blowing on the starboard side, good progress was made.

In the morning the mountain, with its smoke, was far

away in the horizon, and they soon lost sight of it altogether, and the smoke became no more than an ordinary cloud.

The mainland, as Schmitze considered it to be, came into view about noon, and just as it was getting dark they entered the mouth of a small river, and about a mile up brought the boat to a natural landing-stage.

The other portion of the little community was there to give the welcome, and a warm, solid, yet solemn reception was given to all.

As for Hal and Grip, they came in for an ovation, and Hal had to tell the story of his adventures in the mine, omitting only the discovery of the diamonds, as soon as he was safe ashore.

On the morrow, Hal, Grip, and the Great Herr surveyed the country around them.

The next day there was another survey, and far away to the south there was a thin line of smoke, towards which they decided to move.

Schmitze, with a crew of six, was sent to navigate the boat in that direction. The last of the party, with their belongings, moved slowly along the beach.

It was rather tedious to Hal, who presently proposed that he should go on as scout.

Grip had cut his foot that morning while walking among the rocks, owing to the bottom of one of his boots having given out.

The injury was not serious, but the easier movements of the main body suited him better than Hal's quick pace.

Smiling at the idea of any peril, Hal, armed with his rifle, set forward alone.

For a time the beach was the better path, but by-and-bye it became so broken up that he was obliged to make a circuit inland.

After climbing a hill he came to a country that was a mixture of wood and open land and water.

It was such a charming fairyland that he stood for a time contemplating it with delight.

Slowly moving on, he passed through a grove of mahogany trees of enormous size, and in getting clear of it, found himself in another sterile spot.

Placing his gun against a tree, he walked on a little way, intending to climb another tree that stood alone, to look about him.

The smoke of the fire, towards which he had been moving, was no longer in sight.

He sauntered on, making slight detours to avoid huge stones sticking out of the soil.

Suddenly the sound of horse's hoofs fell upon his ears.

Turning his face inland he saw a horseman with a number of wolfish hounds at his heels approaching him.

How well he knew that figure, and that careless, yet safe seat.

It was his brother Louis.

By what strange freak of fate had they again been brought together?

For a moment he was dazed, but Louis, as he approached, showed no signs of astonishment.

On the contrary, he rode straight at Hal, with a savage, determined look in his eyes.

Only for a moment he reined up a little as he drew near.

" Will you ever dog my footsteps ?" he cried. " Am I never to be clear of you ?"

Then he drew a pistol from his belt and fired point-blank at his brother.

Hal felt the sting of a bullet near his shoulder and fell. The savage hounds at that moment came up and turned upon him.

They were like wolves more than dogs, and were evidently half wild. Their looks did not belie them ; they were as ferocious as any beast of the forest.

Louis rode on, disregarding an involuntary cry for help that broke from Hal's lips.

With no other weapon than a stout piece of stick which happened to be lying near Hal gallantly defended himself.

He dealt the first brute a blow that laid him howling on the ground, and then, with a chorus of yelping howls, the others were upon him.

And Louis rode on after another look back, leaving his brother to what he knew was as cruel a fate as could fall to the lot of man.

CHAPTER XXV.

UNWONTED EXERTIONS OF THE GREAT HERR AND HIS
FRIENDS—A DISCOVERY—HAL'S ILLNESS.

HAL felt the teeth of one of the dogs in his left arm, and made a tremendous effort to beat off his furious assailants.

Alone he never could have done it, although with his stout cudgel he brained two of them.

But, happily, his friends had not liked the idea of his going forward alone, and although Grip was unable to increase his pace, the Great Herr and some of his followers put on a wonderful spurt for them, and were not far behind.

Hal had lingered, too, and so enabled them to make up a lot of ground.

They heard the yelps of the dogs and Hal shouting as they dashed out of the wood and came in sight of our hero struggling with his dangerous foes.

Then, startling as it may appear, the Great Herr broke into a RUN.

With such an example before them, what else could his followers do? They also broke into a run.

Half-a-dozen heavily-built men dashed into the pack, and with various weapons soon put all but two *hors de combat*, and the pair who dodged their blows took to their heels and scampered off, yelping with terror.

"Oh! my young friend," said the Great Herr, "vat am dis? Tell me if you am dead."

"I am not hurt much," replied Hal, faintly, "but pretty well pumped out. Thanks for coming so timely to my aid. I have got a bite or two," said Hal, as they helped him up. "It is nothing. It is not the first time I have been bitten by a dog."

There was a spring at hand, and walking there with the assistance of the Great Herr, he washed his wounds and bound them up.

Then they sat down to await the arrival of the others.

Hal could not withhold the story of the base attack made upon him by his brother.

He had borne so much, and the time had come when he could bear no more, so he told all.

The Great Herr was profoundly agitated by the narration.

"He is not to be cured," he said. "Dis broder of yours is all bad; but it is a strange ting that you should always be meeting thus."

"It is what some people call Fate," replied Hal, sadly. "Perhaps, after all, it is not strange. No doubt he was brought here as Schmitze was, by the wind and currents. One thing, however, puzzles me much—he was here on horseback."

"Den dere am settlers here," said the Great Herr.

In half an hour the rest of the party came up, and one of their number having gone to a point that commanded a view of the sea, and reported the boat as coasting along steady and safe, they went forward to look for the settlement.

There was no settlement; but a mile or so away they came in view of a log-house, built upon a piece of rising ground, and near it was fixed a flag-staff, with a line for running up a flag; but the top was bare of this ornament or signal.

Two men were standing by the hut looking seaward. They had evidently espied the boat.

One of these men was Louis Warrington, and the other the last of his band of followers, Cavanat the Frenchman.

The Great Herr recognised both instantly.

"Ah!" he said, "dere are de villains. Let us go on."

For a moment Hal hesitated. Louis was his brother, and he felt now that he could forgive him; but there were the wrongs he had given to the others, and he could not stay their hands.

"Take him, if you can," he said; "I wash my hands of him. But do not forget that he is a desperate fellow."

The quick eyes of Cavanat detected the party a moment later, and he was seen to draw Louis' attention to them.

Immediately both made a dash for a small wooden shed by the side of the house, from which they dragged the horse, that was still saddled.

It was clear that they had no other, and they wished to fly away from their pursuers.

The horse was very restive, and twisted and turned

about, lashing out behind. Neither of the men could mount it.

Suddenly Louis struck it a violent blow across the nose, and, letting go of the bridle, it dashed away. Louis and Cavanat dashed off in the direction of a wood inland, and speedily put themselves out of reach of immediate pursuit.

Hal had been weakened by his recent encounter, and the Herr and his friends were not capable of two sprints in one day, so no further pursuit was attempted.

"Zere is one ting," said the Great Herr, with a smile of satisfaction; "zey have left de horse behind dem."

The first thing to be done was to take possession of that hut, and the second to signal to the boat the fact that the party had come to a halt.

The first led to some strange and unexpected discoveries.

The hut was not that of a common settler, but a building erected for scientific observations of some sort, for the main room in front had a number of beautiful instruments ranged round it.

Nobody there knew the exact use of the majority, but Hal recognised a microscope and a small electric battery among them.

How such things came there was a terrible puzzle to the Great Herr, but Hal knew that the enterprise of countries interested in scientific discoveries led to observatories, big and little, being erected in all parts of the world.

But where were the men to whom these instruments belonged?

Hal grew sick at heart as he thought of the dread possibility—nay, the probability—of his brother and his companion having murdered them.

Grip had the same idea, but he did not give it vent. Nor was there any need for him or Hal to do so.

The Great Herr likewise jumped at the same conclusion.

Without going into any preliminary suggestions he went at once to the matter of their graves.

"I wonder," he said, "where de poor men are buried?"

Before fully inspecting the hut, which was divided into

several rooms, they went wearily in search of the last resting-place of the men all were convinced had been foully slain.

The graves of the men were not found, but the men were.

They had been foully murdered—we spare the reader the ghastly details—and their bodies cast into a hollow a hundred yards from the hut.

They were both Englishmen, of middle age, and they looked like men of learning and refinement ; but a close inspection was impossible, for they had been dead a week or more.

A spade, among other implements in the out-house, which also served as a stable, having been procured, a grave was dug, and the remains of the hapless men laid to rest.

The Great Herr, with reverence, recited as much of the burial service as he knew, and a rough wooden cross was raised to mark the spot.

Those who had been engaged in the service went back to the hut, and were joined by Schmitze, who had brought his boat to an anchor, and had come ashore for instructions.

Meanwhile the women had made another welcome discovery.

In one of the rooms there were stores of things, such as tea, sugar, and flour, and tinned meats—enough perhaps to last the party a week, and were therefore intended to supply the murdered men for much longer.

"They have been left here for a long time," said Hal ; "probably by their own choice. I had hopes that a ship would soon appear to take them away, and so be the means of our own rescue."

"But der am one ting," said the Great Herr, slowly. "Vat if zey say to us, 'You kill dose dead men ; come and hang ?'"

This was a possibility Hal had overlooked.

"But surely they would believe in us ?" he said. "We are so many."

"Zey might," said the Great Herr ; "but, you zee, zey might NOT."

And that much Hal was obliged to admit.

As night came on his wounds became heated, and he was feverish. He tried to hide it, but his watchful friends saw that he was not well.

The Herr's wife prepared him a bed in one of the rooms, and another was given up to the women and children. The men were told to sleep where they could.

Some elected to go and sleep in the boat, others had the big room to lie down in, and a third portion were set to watch during the night, in case Louis Warrington should be daring enough to return.

Judging by his daring in the past it was not all improbable.

At midnight Hal was in a high fever, and by his side sat Grip and the Great Herr.

Among other things they had found in the store-room were a few simple medicines—among them a bottle of quinine, which is good for fever.

The Great Herr gave him a dose, but it had no apparent effect. Hal got worse and worse.

For a time neither of the watchers gave vent to what was in their minds; but at last Grip blurted out—

"Can this be that awful hydrophobia?"

And the Great Herr, folding his hands across his breast, said, reverently—

"Let us pray not, and, if it is, ve must leave him to Heaven. As I zee dese tings, ze fever have come too soon for dat; but I do not know."

CHAPTER XXVI.

A WEEK LATER—GRIP'S RESOLVE.

SEVEN days passed, and there was rejoicing among the party of adventurers gathered about the hut.

Hal had not been suffering from the most dreaded of all diseases, but a fever arising from fatigue, mental excitement, and exposure.

A little medicine and the watchful care of loving friends had brought him through it, leaving him very weak.

The treasure he had acquired Grip took care of during

his illness, and when the worst was over he restored it to him at once.

"I don't feel comfortable with that, Master Hal," he said ; "it's too heavy for me."

But now that Hal had sufficiently recovered to need only ordinary care, and Grip had got the better of his accident, the latter proceeded to put into execution a grim resolve he had formed.

He confided it to the Great Herr, but not to Hal.

"Tell him when I am clear away," he said. "I know if I asked his leave he would say no, for, in spite of all his wrongs, he would forgive him still."

"But ze man he forgive," said the Great Herr ; "ze man his broder is indeed ?"

"It is so," said Grip. "I've got no right to be his judge perhaps, but I'll be so for Master Hal's sake, even if it costs me the love he bears an old and faithful servant."

His voice was a little husky as he thought of this bare possibility, but he was resolved. He would hunt out Louis Warrington, capture him if possible, and carry out the sentence passed upon him by the Great Herr.

He was led to the resolve by the discovery that Louis and his companions were not far away.

They had been seen by scouts, sent to look round the country, skulking about inland, rifle in hand, probably in search of game.

Where they lived was not very clear, but, far as the eye could see, there was no hut or sign of civilisation around.

The absence of all natives, too, pointed to its being an uninhabited part of the globe.

At the head of the flagstaff outside the hut there now fluttered a red flag, which had been found.

It was hoisted with the hope of attracting some passing ship, but hitherto no sail appeared in sight.

Grip had never any love for Louis, even prior to the development of his inborn delight in evil, and the faithful follower of Hal had long hoped for an opportunity to bring to book the author of so much suffering.

Now an opportunity offered itself he would not throw it away.

Let us now see what the two fugitive villains are doing. Hard times had come upon them.

A cave was their home, and their means of subsistence very precarious.

They had rifles, but only a few rounds of ammunition, and when the latter was exhausted grim starvation would not be far off.

Louis had in his possession the diamonds of which he had robbed the Great Herr.

Cavanat had often urged that they should be divided, and each take his portion.

In case they became separated both would have the wherewithal to be fairly rich in any place where they could be disposed of.

Meanwhile they were of no service whatever.

Behold them in the light of the early morning sitting at the mouth of their cave gloomily reviewing their position.

"For mine own part," said Cavanat, "I would go to ze inland."

"And die like dogs?" replied Louis. "Don't I tell you that I read enough in the papers of those men we—he stopped as if a word choked him—"you know what I mean. It was enough to learn that this is a wild, uninhabited region, and our only chance is to keep near the coast and wait some passing vessel."

"But you are not near ze coast;" growled Cavanat.

"We will go there again," muttered Louis, "when those fools have moved on."

"Zey will leave nothing but ze empty hut."

"Well, to the hut somebody will come soon. You and me can tell a tale of having found it empty, and of traces of that gang who, no doubt, murdered—that's the word—those two old dunderheads who were so glad to see us. and so shocked to find what blackguards we were."

CHAPTER XXVII.

IN PURSUIT OF LOUIS AND CAVANAT.

"AH! they vas so," said Cavanat, with a chuckle. "And zey say—'Go, or ve set de dogs on you.' Ah! ve vent, but in ze night it is back ve come, and—"

"There, that will do," muttered Louis; "it wasn't a pleasant job, but it's done now, and it can't be called back. They would have taken care of us if we had behaved ourselves. It's bitter to think of our lot, hungry as wolves, with plenty to buy all sorts of luxuries, and yet nothing to eat."

"Hush !" said Cavanat.

"Well, what's the matter now ?" grumbled Louis.

"Footsteps; can't you hear them ?"

Louis sprang to his feet, and peered over the rugged rocks at the mouth of the cave.

An exclamation of anger and bitterness escaped him.

"That Grip," he said, "and a gang of those rough Germans. Give me my rifle. We must clear out of this."

Cavanat hurriedly brought out his rifle, and the pair, slipping round the side of the cave, plunged into a veritable jungle of undergrowth and stunted trees.

The movement was a quick one, but it was seen by Grip.

He did not shout, but quickly directed his men to go in pursuit.

Spreading out into a line with about six feet between each man they started.

Not a word was uttered, but they could not avoid marking their progress with the crash of rotten twigs with which their path was thickly strewn.

Louis and the Frenchman heard them, and heaping anathemas on the heads of their pursuers fought on through bushes that grew thicker and thicker until they were well nigh impassable.

Behind them they left a trail which Grip soon picked up and followed with the eager haste of a sleuth hound to find, when the jungle which covered about a hundred acres, had been traversed, that Louis and Cavanat had got a good quarter of a mile start, and were running across the plain in the direction of a small stream.

On the other side of it lay a wild country of rock, wood, and hill, which would afford them a shelter from which it would be difficult to dislodge them; but Grip did not give up the chase.

His practised eye saw where the river rippled in the shallows, and where it sometimes showed a depth of water which would compel the men to swim.

The ford was lower down, nearer the pursuers, and by a quick movement they might intercept the fugitives.

Half-a-dozen words apprised his men of his intention, and they exerted themselves to their utmost to carry out his desire.

But the wary Louis was on the watch, and interpreting the nature of the movement, suddenly abandoned the idea of crossing the stream, at that point, at least, and bore away to the left towards the coast.

By this movement he gained ground, and both he and the Frenchman were more vigorous in running than Grip or his footmen.

They speedily distanced them, and were finally lost.

They disappeared into a wood that ran nearly down to the sea, touching the stream about two miles from the hut.

Grip pulled up, for he himself and followers were all pretty well blown.

But the chase was not by any means given up.

As soon as they had recovered their second wind, which every athlete knows is more enduring than the first, they set forward again, and struck the trail again near the wood.

The ground here was rather soft, being swampy from a recent overflow of the river, and every footstep left its mark.

On entering the wood, the ground was drying, but it was soft enough to leave the trail of Louis and Cavanat clear enough for a child to follow.

But the wood sloped upward, and the trail grew fainter until it was lost.

This, however, was not until the termination of the wood was reached.

The eager men run out, and found themselves on the summit of a cliff, which a few yards on went down sheer to a shingly beach below.

Right and left, the ground was much too open for anyone to hide, and the inference was that the quarry had pushed back into the wood.

They searched up and down, but found no traces of foot-steps. They spent hours in the search, and found nothing to guide them.

At last Grip entered the wood on one side, and struck right across in a way would lead to the discovery of any trail.

But there was none, except those made in passing through.

They then examined the trees, to see if the men were hiding in the branches, making excursions to the cliff every now and then, to see if the men were in sight.

But all their strenuous efforts remained unrewarded.

It was noon when they threw themselves down on the cliffs to rest, and to partake of some of the food they had brought with them.

It was a bitter disappointment to Grip, who had felt pretty sure of success.

He still kept on the alert, with ears for every sound in the wood, and his eyes watching the beach, his men eating their food in glum silence.

"He was always a devil," said Grip at last. "As a boy, people used to call him the Pretty Imp—he played such pranks and was so artful in anything he did; but I will have him. I won't go back without him."

This was rather a rash resolution; but Grip meant what he said, and he had the dogged nature that over-comes a thousand difficulties where a weaker resolution would fall.

He would not go back, and did not go back, until he found what he sought.

But the manner of the finding was very different to what he expected.

That Louis and his companions had passed back through the woods he did not now believe.

They had gone up the beach or cliff to the right; for to go to the left would lead them back to the hut, and Louis, with all his daredevilry, would never dream of doing that.

Their way lay, then, up the cliff; and, having refreshed and rested themselves, the dogged pursuers began their search anew.

CHAPTER XXVIII.

GRIP RENEWS THE SEARCH—HE IS THE WITNESS OF
A STRANGE SCENE—HAL IS SENT FOR.

THOSE who persevere generally succeed in the end.
That is an accepted proverb among those who have any
knowledge of life. Whether Grip was aware of it or not
he persevered.

With his band of followers he pursued his way along
the cliff, and speedily came to an obstacle that threatened
to stop his progress in that direction.

It was a rent in the cliff, like a split in a log, running
rom the stone some distance inland further than Grip
could see.

So clean was it that the sides of the rent were as per-
pendicular as walls, and the only visible way of getting
down was to be very precipitate and jump, which would
be a case of certain death.

The cliff itself on the sea-side was also very steep, but
practicable to a sure-footed man.

Grip felt that with his experience he could make the
descent, but what of his followers?

They were all heavy-footed, slow-moving men, and
when he put the question to them they all said it was impossible.

"We are sure to fall," they said.

To go back would result in a great loss of time, but
there seemed to be nothing else to do, and Grip was about
to give the order when he saw something below which
fairly took his breath away.

It was Louis and Cavanat cautiously creeping among
the broken rocks behind.

That they did not see Grip about was clear, for neither
looked up, but occasionally cast a glance behind, no
doubt expecting the pursuers in that direction.

Grip, with a motion of his hand, waved his followers
back, and the action also expressed his desire for them to
be as quiet as possible.

They drew back, and Grip, having taken off his hat,
lay down and peered over the cliff.

His object was to watch Louis and Cavanat to a hiding-place, which they were probably seeking.

Louis was moving on in front, and the Frenchman a few feet behind.

They moved with the utmost caution, dodged in and out among the rocks, and crawling on their hands and knees across open spaces.

Proceeding in this way, they came right under Grip, and then an extraordinary and terrible thing took place.

Cavanat suddenly leaped upon his companion and stabbed him in the back. Louis fell forward on his face, and his false comrade dealt him another blow with the knife that glittered in his hand.

Then he turned Louis over, and to all appearance he was dead.

Cavanat's next step was to search his clothes, and while he was doing this Grip, unable to contain himself, summarily avenged the foul murder.

The rifle he carried was loaded, and taking careful aim, he fired.

Cavanat leaped up, ran like a greyhound for a score yards, then fell upon the sands and rolled over and over, fought and bit like a mad beast, and finally, with his face downwards, lay still.

"Go back," said Grip, rising and addressing his followers. "Tell my master to come here at once, and to come along by the shore."

The men hurried off with but an imperfect idea of what had happened.

Of one thing only were they sure, and that was Grip had shot somebody below.

It was only natural they should assume that Grip had shot Louis, and that was the story they took back with them.

Grip began his descent, and had to proceed warily, for the projections available offered him but an insecure foot-hold.

No accident befell him, however, and he reached the sands in safety.

Glancing at Cavanat, and seeing that he had not moved,

Grip was assured that his shot had been fatal; then he turned his attention to Louis.

The wanton, reckless brother of Hal was not dead; there were signs of faint breathing, and the colour had not wholly forsaken his cheeks..

Grip raised him up and saw that his wounds had ceased to bleed or were bleeding very slowly, so he dragged him gently to a small sand-bank and laid him there.

There was little in Louis' life to excite sympathy, but now that the hand of death was upon him Grip's animosity came to an end.

It was horrible to think of dying thus by the hand of one who had been his friend, or, at least, boon companion in evil.

Cupidity led to the crime.

Cavanat coveted the jewels Louis had in his possession, and, believing, moreover, that the chances of one escaping were better than with two together, he had resolved to commit the dastardly crime.

Swift and sure had been his reward.

Trickling down the face of the cliff was a tiny thread of water, part of the drainings of the distant marshy wood. Grip collected a little of the water in his hand, and with it he moistened Louis' lips and forehead.

In a few moments he opened his eyes and stared at Grip, but without any signs of recognition.

"It's an awful thing, Cavanat," he said, feebly, "to be hunted like a dog."

"It isn't Cavanat," replied Grip. "Don't you know me?"

"Know you? Of course I do," replied Louis. "You are that thief of a lawyer who has got hold of our estate!"

So he talked when spoken to, and when Grip was silent he rambled on about scenes of the past, some of them not pleasant to listen to.

Grip at intervals fetched him water.

In a little while he began to get better. His head became clearer, and at length the events of the immediate past became clearer to him.

"Ha!" he said, suddenly. "You are Grip."

"Yes," replied Grip. "I am glad you know me."

"Who was it struck me down—you?" asked Louis.

"No; it was that Frenchy fellow who was with you," replied Grip.

"Cavanat?'

Grip nodded.

Louis raised his hand with an effort and let it fall upon his breast. He had not the strength to place it firmly there.

His eager fingers soon discovered the bag; his stolen treasure was safe.

"Grip," he said, "are you alone?"

"Yes," replied Grip.

"Where is my brother?"

"I've sent for him. But he isn't very strong; perhaps you can tell why. I hope he will soon be here."

A shadow passed over Louis' face.

"What a mad, senseless, heartless brute I've been, Grip," he said.

Grip said nothing. To deny it would be too palpable a lie, though it might be to soften the last moments of a dying man.

"I think I MUST have been mad," said Louis, after a silence. "But the end has come; I've done the work of the devil, and my wages will soon be paid. I should like to see Hal, if only for a moment. But he must be quick. Can you see him coming?'

"I can't see far," replied Grip, "for there's so many rocks about the shore."

"I suppose you have nothing stronger than water?" replied Louis.

Grip shook his head.

"Ah! well, a little more of that; it's better than nothing."

Grip brought him water from that time every few minutes for an hour or more, and then he saw Hal and the Great Herr approaching.

CHAPTER XXIX.

THE LAST INTERVIEW BETWEEN THE BROTHERS—
LOUIS' REQUEST—BACK TO THE OBSERVATORY—A
SAIL.

HAL was too weak to walk very fast, and so the Great
Herr had been able to keep up with them.

As Hal drew near his eyes were first directed to his
brothers and then fixed on Grip.

"I would rather," he said, "that any other hand but
yours had done this."

"Master Hal," replied Grip, "I've not touched him;
I've naught to do with it. Yonder lies the man that tried
to take his life; I've killed him."

"This is a great relief to me, Grip," said Hal. "Forgive me. I was told that you had shot my brother."

He was now near Louis, and turned upon him a kindly,
pitying look.

In Louis' face was a world of repentance, humiliation,
and despair.

Thus had the brothers come together for the last time.

"Hal," said Louis, feebly, "are you not glad to see
me brought down at last?"

"No, Louis," answered Hal. "It is only a terrible
awakening from an ugly dream. Oh! Louis—Louis, we
were never brothers in life; but now I trust the tie of
blood will not be wholly forgotten."

"After all I have done to you? And you forgive me

"Heaven knows I do."

The expression of Louis' face was very pitiful.

"I could have borne hard words and even blows bette
than this. If you had raised your hand to find a deeper
revenge you would have failed; your forgiveness crushes
me."

"You would not have me withdraw it, Louis?"

"No, Hal. Ah! what a monster I have been; but
you know the legend of our family—about every ten
generations a monster was to be born into it, the last to
wreck the home? I am that last, Hal. In me all that
has been bad in our race existed; it will die with me."

Now, for the first time, he became aware of the presence

of the Great Herr, and a faint smile played for a moment about his lips.

"So you are here, my simple friend," he said. "I robbed you, who had been so good. And can you forgive?"

"It is so," said the Great Herr, solemnly.

"All that I took is here," said Louis, pointing to his breast. "You can take it now if you will."

The Great Herr, with a motion of his hand, dissented.

"Then take it when I am gone," said Louis. "It won't be long before you will have your own. Hal, in me expires the ill blood of our race; in you the name will revive. Good-bye! If you do not loathe me too much to touch my hand—"

Hal stooped and took his right hand between his own.

"You forgive me?" said Louis.

"I do," answered Hal.

"With all your heart?"

"With all my heart."

"Then, once more, Good—bye!"

There was a heaving of his chest, a brightening of the eye which quickly faded, a sob, then the deadly rattle in the throat, that betrayed the arrival of the conqueror of all men—King Death.

In a few moments the spirit of wild Louis Warrington had fled.

.   •   •   •   •   •   •   •

They buried the two dead men, many feet apart, upon the sands when the tide went out, and so gave them graves o'er which many an angry sea would roll, and no man from thenceforth tell where they were laid.

"It is better so," said Hal, "for I would have all record of my mad brother hidden away and forgotten."

"Ah! zen," said the Great Herr, "he VAS mad?"

"Yes," replied Hal; "but there was a method and system in it that made him amenable to the laws of his country. He was not mad in the sense in which the world would view his acts, but what else could he be? Once rich and the owner of a good estate, with friends, youth, and health, he deliberately squanders all in a few short years, and brings himself to the end witnessed. Yes, Herr, he was mad."

"You are indeed a brother," was all the Great Herr said.

For three days after this closing scene of a stormy life there was a quietude in the observatory.

All were in need of rest, but it could not last for long as there was little left to eat, and something had to be done to stave off the semi-starvation that threatened them.

Men and women require something more than fish to subsist upon, and to fish they were now practically reduced.

Plans were on the board for snaring or shooting some of the wild animals that had been seen in the plains, when one morning a sail was seen on the horizon.

As soon as the look-out had shouted the glad news the whole community were upon the cliff, all straining their eager eyes to make out the course it was taking.

There it was, a mere speck, and a mere speck it remained for some time, creeping along the horizon.

Then it began to diminish, and soon had almost entirely disappeared.

Stifled groans burst from the men; the women began to sob.

It was hard to see the star of hope rising only to set at once again.

But it did not wholly disappear.

Nor did it decrease in size, but gradually began to swell again, and without moving along the horizon.

"She is standing in !" cried Hal.

And then from the throats of the men there burst a ringing cheer, and the signal-flag, which was kept flying throughout the day, was lowered half-mast and drawn up again many times, with the hope that its shifting would catch the eye of those on board.

Nearer came the vessel, until the hull could be seen and the outline of each sail distinguished by those with good eyesight—nearer, nearer, until there could be no doubt that the signal was seen.

Then she bore away a bit, and a boat was lowered.

Now indeed were the poor wanderers frantic with delight.

If but it should prove to be a ship Europe-bound—no matter what port—all their troubles might be considered over.

The boat contained half-a-dozen men and an officer—a cheery young fellow, who leaped ashore and was met by Hal, who saw at once that he was an Englishman.

The ship was the Lion King, homeward bound to Liverpool in ballast, after discharging a cargo at various places on the African coast.

Part of her ballast was gold, but the young officer did not say anything about that.

He was amazed to find so many people on that desolate coast, and when he heard the story about the two men murdered in the observatory he became dubious, and said he could do nothing without consulting his captain.

So he returned to the Lion King, and another time of anxiety ensued.

At last the vessel began to approach the shore, and when an anchorage was found the anchor was lowered and the sails furled.

When that was done, the boat returned again, bringing the captain.

He was a portly man, with a good-humoured face, and introduced himself, giving his name as Manders.

Leaving his men with the boat, he went up to the observatory and examined it thoroughly.

Hal showed him the instruments and some note-books which had been found, which proved that the two strange men were Englishmen taking observations for the King of Belgium, who had fitted them out and commissioned them to examine that lone land.

"We must get everything on board," said Captain Manders, "and I shall hand you over to the authorities when we get home. For my own part, I will say this much, that I believe your story of the ruffians having killed these unfortunate gentlemen ; but you will understand I cannot be your witness, and I do not wish to be your judge.'

He was kind enough in his manner, but he made it perfectly clear that he meant to have the whole thing investigated.

He was not told that one of the murderers was Hal's brother.

It was not thought necessary to go so far; and when he asked where the graves of the two men were, the reply rather astonished him.

"Why could you not bury them where they could, if necessary, be found?" he asked.

And to this there was no reply, save that it was considered easier to bury them in the sand.

To this answer Captain Manders said little.

"It is not my affair," he said. "If you satisfy the people at home, I shall have no complaint to make."

"Surely they will take the word of so many?" said Hal.

"I hope so," said the captain.

Hal then changed the subject to that of the expense of transporting so many people across the ocean.

He expressed himself as willing to meet it by paying on his return home.

"You are a rich man in the old country, then?" said the captain, grimly.

"I am rich enough to pay all moderate demands," replied Hal.

The Lion King was a vessel of about eight hundred tons burden. It had a cabin fitted up for about half-a-dozen passengers, although, as a rule, it did not carry any. Now and then merchants and other men going to out-of-the-way ports had availed themselves of her as a means of transport. This cabin was given up to the women and children, and accommodation for the men was made elsewhere.

They did not linger in that lone land while making arrangements. As soon as the instruments and all portable things had been got on board the anchor was hoisted.

Schmitze wept at parting with the old boat, which perforce had to be left behind. Captain Manders was asked to allow it to be tethered to the stern of the ship, and wed in the wake of his vessel.

"Oh! no," he said. "It would be like dragging an anchor. When do you think I should get into port?"

So the old boat was left beached in the deserted country, there to rot or be knocked to pieces by the waves, as the wind and water might decide.

And now to Hal there was an opening into a new life aboard.

He did not fear the result of the investigation into the death of the two hapless scientists, for how could any sane tribunal doubt the story which would be told by so many?

CHAPTER XXX.

LANDING AT LIVERPOOL—OFFICIAL ENQUIRY—HAL HEARS NEWS WHICH HE THINKS MAY INTEREST HIM.

HAL thought most of what he would do with his wealth when he *got* home.

As yet he had no correct idea of the value of the jewels he carried in his bosom, but he knew it must be very considerable, and his great longing now was to recover the family estate and do his best to restore the family name.

That he had an up-hill task before him he knew, but hope is a bright star which gives both light and life to a man.

All on board were happy. Their wanderings had come to an end, and there was only one there with a sad thought in his head.

That was Hal.

Clara had never left his thoughts for long, and now, in the hour of joy, he wondered what had been her fate.

Louis, dying, had not named her, and there seemed no probability of his having any knowledge of her or her friends.

Perhaps the patriarch and those with them had followed Hal inland, but on their way had fallen a prey to the savages.

It was hard to tell, and all that Hal could do was to

Quick as thought Hal had him by the throat.

wait until he arrived home, and then by any means in his power endeavour to ascertain what had befallen them.

What these means were to be he could only guess, but then again came hope to comfort him.

"She is not dead," he said.   "We shall meet again !"

.   .   .   .

It was a clear autumn day when the good ship that had done such excellent service dropped her anchor at Liverpool.

Before landing his passengers Captain Manders went ashore, and made a communication to the authorities respecting the murder of the injured occupants of the observatory, and the police took the matter in hand.

They came on board, heard what the passengers had to say, and concluded that the story was an honest one.

But they would not as yet permit them to go out of the district, although they allowed them to go ashore with the understanding that they were under police supervision, and would be arrested the instant they attempted to get away.

The men alone were embraced by this intimation from the authorities ; the women and children were at liberty to leave, if they were so inclined, but, of course, they elected to stay.

"Ve have noting to fear," said the Great Herr ; "so ve remain, and smoke our pipes in peace."

The question of finance now arose, and Hal wrote at once to the family lawyer of the Warringtons, asking for one of the firm or a confidential clerk to be sent to him.

"I have the means of recovering the old house" (he wrote), *"if it is in the market, or if the present owner will part with it."*

Within forty-eight hours Mr. Dowland, a junior member of the firm, was in Liverpool, and was entertained and amazed by the story Hal had to tell him.

When it came to the point of the diamonds he examined the stones, and declared his belief that they were genuine and very valuable.

He wrote a cheque for the present use of Hal and hi'

friends, and, taking a few of the stones with him, he returned to town.

Hal, with Grip, meanwhile put up at an hotel, and the others got lodgings round about. The next day a wire was sent to Hal—

" Right!   The very best."

That sufficed, and Hal knew that he was rich—much richer than a Warrington had been for several generations.

But still caution had to be exercised before he attempted to realise his property.

While the officials withheld their unqualified belief in his story he had better say nothing about it ; and officials work by slow methods.

Days passed, and the word proclaiming his entire freedom was still withheld.

Having nothing to do, he and Grip wandered about the town and the docks, amusing themselves by watching the busy life of active Liverpool, and it was whilst they were thus engaged that they were waylaid by a local reporter in search of something for his paper.

He had heard something of the story of the rescue in an indirect manner, and he now came to the fountain-head for further information.

Hal saw no reason to withhold anything, save the possession of the diamonds, and he old his interviewer the whole story.

" It is similar to one I heard of about six weeks ago," the reporter said. " A vessel—it was the Evening Star, I think. It had picked up a small party from an island in the same latitude. They were Russians—an old man, his daughter and son, and another."

Hal was startled by this intelligence. Was it possible that it was his old friends who had thus been rescued?

" Did you see these people ?" he asked.

" Oh ! yes," replied the reporter ; " I interviewed them. The name of three of them was—well, I forget for the moment—and the daughter was remarkably beautiful."

" What became of them ?" asked Hal, assuming an indifference he did not feel.

"They settled somewhere in the town—the father, son, and daughter.   The other man took passage on a ship for America, working his way over.   Let me see; I heard somebody speaking about them the other day.   I was told they were in a sorry plight."

"Is there any possibility of discovering their present address?" asked Hal.

He spoke low to conceal his agitation.   The reporter shrugged his shoulders.

"Liverpool is a big place," he said, "and we have two populations—a stationary and a floating one."

"I have reason to believe that I have some slight knowledge of these people," said Hal, "and would willingly pay for more information concerning them.   Can you help me?"

"I can try," was the answer; "but the police will be more likely to give you information.   However, leave it to me until to-morrow.   Where are you staying?"

Hal gave him the name of his hotel, and after having had a glass of wine together they parted.

Hal did not rest idle until the morning, but went about making enquiries in every direction.

He came across many people who had seen or heard of the party rescued, but nobody knew what had become of them.

"We have so much going on here," one man said, "that affairs of that sort are soon forgotten."

Hal returned to his hotel at a later hour and went to bed.   Sleep refused to come to him until half the night was passed, and he was in sound repose at ten o'clock when Grip came into his room and announced the arrival of the reporter.

"Does he bring me any news?" asked Hal.

"He LOOKS as if he does," replied Grip.

This was enough.

Hal tumbled out of bed, dressed himself with all speed, and went down to the coffee-room, where he found the reporter reading the morning paper.

"You see, Mr. Warrington," he said, "I have made nearly a column out of you.   'Remarkable Rescue,' 'Strange repetition of a strange story.'   Don't you see?"

Hal glanced at the paragraph, and smiled.

"Excuse me," he said, "I am more interested in my friends at present than in myself. Have you heard any news of them?"

"Yes," replied the reporter; "I have raked them out. Excuse the expression. They are in a bad way—being literally on the verge of starvation in Bingley's-rents. I had a difficulty in getting at the true state of the case, for they bear their lot like many people—in silence."

"If it is indeed my friends," said Hal, "I shall not be able to sufficiently reward you."

"As for reward," replied the reporter, "I am not such an ass as to say that I won't take it; but at the same time, unless you can well afford it, I do not want anything. I shall make another par out of it, anyway."

"If you can show me where Bingley's-rents are," said Hal, "we will go at once."

"Softly. Have you had any breakfast?"

"Not yet."

"Then have some. You will want it. Nature insists upon having her full amount of refreshment"

Hal saw the wisdom of the remark, and ordered breakfast for two at once—Grip had partaken of his an hour before.

The meal was got through as quickly as possible, and the reporter and Hal set forth.

Through broad thoroughfares, narrow streets, alleys, and strange short cuts the reporter led his eager companion, until they came to what was undoubtedly one of the poorest parts of the town.

There, in a blind street, was a row of houses called Bingley's-rents.

Little need was there for anyone to enquire into the pecuniary condition of the inhabitants. The grim seal of poverty was on everything—the houses, the roadway, and on the children in the street.

Miserable looking men came out of some of the houses, and, with their hands in their pockets, sauntered away.

"No work to do" was written on their faces, and the half-dozen women who stood at the doors, listless. and for the most part silent, had the look of those without a prospect or a hope.

As for the little children in the roadway, playing as children will play even if the plague is around them, Hal's heart bled for the little ones.

Such wan faces, pinched forms, and ragged garbs he had never seen before.

He offered to some as he passed by the loose pence and small silver he had in his pocket, and they stared at him as if he had been a spirit from the clouds.

They did not thank him. Having had so few opportunities of thanking anyone for a kindness *they did not know how to do it.*

This may read like a fable; but we know, and many know, that in all our great cities there are children so long neglected and forlorn that a kindness comes to them like a flash of lightning from the blue sky.

They hardly know what it means.

But they grasped the fact that they had for once in their lives got hold of some money, and raced away with a score of ragged companions at their heels, to spend it at some cheap provision shop.

"Ah! sir," said the reporter, "if you had a purse as deep as the sea, you could empty it among these unfortunates, and still leave some in the cold."

Stopping, he pointed to a house at the other end of the row—the most dilapidated of them all—he said—

"You will find your friends,—if they are your friends—in that dismal place, on the topmost floor. Don't stand on ceremony. Go in—the door is never locked—and walk right up the stairs until you can go no further. Then knock at the nearest door."

"What will you do?" asked Hal.

"Wait for you here," was the reply. "Don't hurry; I have little to do this morning."

With a palpitating heart Hal approached the door.

The door was ajar, and, pushing it open, he went in.

A man in the passage was in the act of lighting his pipe, and drew aside to let him pass. He did not so much as look at him.

Up the stairs, half-rotted by neglect and damp, Hal went warily.

In a room on the first floor a woman was railing at a man for having spent his money in drink, and the man, with a bitter oath, dealt her a blow.

Hal heard it ; but the woman did not scream.

She fell heavily against the door, and merely returned the curse.

" Clara HERE !" thought Hal, with a shudder. " Is it possible ? And, if left here, would she come down to *that* level ?"

Hal hurried up to the next floor, where the hammering of a cobbler broke the quietude.

Then up another short flight of stairs, and the end of his journey was reached.

On the right was the door, and somebody was softly moving about on the other side of it.

He knocked.

The sound in the room ceased, and, after a short silence, whispering followed.

Then the heavy tread of a man, and the door opened.

" Felix !"

" Hal !"

As the two men recognised each other, a short, sharp cry was heard in the room, and Felix, dashing back, caught his sister as she fell.

The shock had overcome her.

Hal saw her—oh! so pale and wan, but beautiful still—and he longed to hold her in his arms, but delicacy kept him at the door.

" Come in," said Felix, hoarsely ; " let me have a good look at you, or I shall think it is a dream."

Hal entered and found himself in a room with a few poor articles of furniture in it, but everything scrupulously neat and clean.

There was a door open at the end and the foot of a poor bed visible.

" Who is it ? What is it ?" asked a feeble voice from the inner room.

" A friend," replied Felix. " Be patient, father Clara—Clara ! Come ; it will not do to give way."

He placed her in a chair, and she soon gave signs of recovering. Hal stood by with one of her hands in his.

"Thank Heaven!" he said, "it is indeed you."

"But how came you here?" asked Felix.

"Clara is coming to," said Hal. "I will tell you my story by-and-bye."

Clara opened her eyes, shuddered, and closed them again.

"It is a vision," she said.

"No, indeed," replied Hal; "I am living, and have returned rich. I only needed this meeting to make my happiness complete."

"It is you, Hal?"

"Yes, dearest."

Once more she opened her eyes and looked at him with a yearning expression. He stooped down and put his lips to her forehead.

"My darling," he said, "all is well with me now."

"But how could you know we were here," said Clara, "as we have concealed our very name?"

"It looks like the work of a magician, doesn't it?" said Hal. "But it is not. Providence has guided me here to do something for those I have a reason to love most dearly. Is your father here?"

"Yes," said Clara; "but he is ill, and we are poor. He has need of things we cannot get for him."

"And which these hands of mine could not earn for him," said Felix, bitterly. "There is no room for men like me in this great hive."

"It matters not now," said Hal. "Let me see your father, but first tell him that I am alive."

"Come in!" said the patriarch from within. "I know your voice Welcome, dear friend and son."

They all went into the other room where the patriarch lay upon his couch. He was terribly thin and white, but the light of joy was in his eyes.

"It gladdens my poor eyes," he said; "you whom we gave up for dead."

"I live, and let that suffice for the present," said Hal. "My first thought must be to take you from this place to where you can have better air. Do not let your pride come in now, for 1 am rich, and I hope one day to be your son, unless Clara has changed the love she once bore me."

Clara turned away, but she extended her hand to him, and he clasped it in his own.

"We are one family," he said. "Is it not so?"

"It is a dream of joy and hope," said the patriarch.

"Felix," said Hal, "come out with me, and let us confer together about what ought to be done. Clara, for a little awhile, Good-bye!"

"Come back soon," she said, "for I cannot yet fully realise that it is indeed you."

CHAPTER XXXI.

FELIX TELLS HIS STORY.

HAL's first care was to see the reporter and assure him that he had indeed found his friends, including Felix by name.

"We owe to you," said Hal, "our happy meeting."

"It isn't much to owe," replied the reporter. "I made a few enquiries in likely places, and ascertained what you wanted. Now, if you will excuse me, I will get about my business."

He had the good sense to see that the two friends would be better by themselves, and was moving off when Hal followed and whispered a few words.

"Oh! it doesn't matter," he said.

"But it does matter," said Hal. "You must let me know where to find you."

"My name is Cranbourne, and you can hear of me at the office of the paper. Good-bye!"

He hurried off to escape any further controversy on the matter.

Hal returned to Felix.

"The first thing to do," said Hal, "is to send a few necessaries to your father and Clara. What is most needed?"

"Everything," said Felix, sadly. "You came just in time; we are positively penniless. For the present a little bread and wine will suffice. You know what frugal people we are."

In a little thoroughfare they found a provision-store, and a basket of necessaries was despatched to the invalid and Clara.

Then Hal led Felix into a restaurant and ordered luncheon for two.

"Now tell me your story, Felix," he said. "How was it you thought we were dead?"

"If you remember," said Felix, "you left us for a day or so, and we expected you to return on the morrow. The next day we became anxious, and I was sent in search of you. Ere I had gone far I found signs of savages, and came across several dead bodies. There were indications of a struggle, too, and the impression was that you had been killed or made captive.

"The latter was a forlorn hope, and I returned to my people, after looking about for two days and seeing several small parties of natives in the war-path. What else could I think but that you were dead?"

"It was very natural," replied Hal.

"I went back despairing," resumed Felix, "and poor Clara was quite prostrated by the dismal tidings I took back with me. The next day a ship came in sight, an English vessel, the Orion, and sent a boat ashore for water. They found us, and offered to take us away. Clara urged us to remain until you returned; but the officers of the Orion assured us there was little hope—none, indeed—and when the time came for us to accept or refuse their offer, what else could we do but accept?

"The captain was kind to us, and gave us a few hours' grace to have a last look around. Clara and I scaled the highest point of the cliff, so that we commanded a view of a large tract of country. All we saw were bands of prowling savages, and we gave you up for lost. Poor Clara—she lingered to the last, and was carried senseless on board. We all grieved most bitterly."

"You did what was right," said Hal. "It was only by sheer good luck that we got away. I will tell you my story by-and-bye, when Clara and your father can listen to it. You left me a suit of clothes. Why was that?"

"Ah! that was our forgetfulness," said Felix. "We left them where they were put shortly after we landed.

Had we thought there were any chance of your returning none of us would have come away."

Felix's story and the luncheon came to an end at the same time, and Hal returned alone to his hotel to make arrangements for the reception of his friends.

There a welcome relief was awaiting him in the form of a letter from the chief of the police, informing him he was at liberty to go where he pleased.

A few minutes afterwards the Great Herr came in, being himself the bearer of similar tidings.

He embraced Hal in the most fatherly manner.

"It is vell," he said; "all is peace. I takes my peoples avay, and tell dem zat dey are not poor. We shall go to Germany, where ze living is sheap, and it is a country I like zo. But before ve go ve have a big supper togezzer."

Hal assented, and then he told him of the discovery he had made, so that the eyes of the Great Herr came quite out of his head, and for a few seconds seemed separated from his body.

"It is vonderful," he said—"vonderful; but all tings is vonderful—our lives, vat ve do and see. It is a great vorld."

There was no need now for Hal to take rooms for his friends at Liverpool. The sooner they were away the better.

So he proposed that the "great supper" should take place that night, and the Herr accepted on behalf of himself and friends.

"If I say zo, it is zo," he said.

And so it was.

They would just as soon have thought of putting their heads under a cart-wheel as refuse an invitation accepted for them by the Great Herr.

We need not describe that supper. It was a great feeding and drinking festivity. The toasts were numerous, and when the time for parting came there was much shaking of hands and some weeping.

"But it is not for ever we part," said the Great Herr. "Ve shall meet again. Good-bye—good-bye!"

Hal had yet one more longing, and that was to run

down to the Heath, and see if the strange old woman who had foretold his destiny was yet alive.

Settled for a time in rooms of his own, and his friends in apartments not far away, he had with the assistance of his lawyer disposed of uncut diamonds sufficient to realise sixty thousand pounds, and only a third of his treasure was gone.

The family estate was not in the market, but it might shortly be, for Jason Ferrell, having lost his father, had become as wild as any of the madcaps with whom he used to associate for business purposes.

He was "going the pace" every way, and if his money lasted another year his constitution would not.

Meanwhile Hal could wait.

He had no love for Ferrell, of course—how could he have?—but he did not desire the man's death.

Once more he would go down to the Heath, and on his return establish a temporary home, and make Clara mistress of it.

Grip, on hearing of his intention, desired to go also.

Hal had often wondered who or what she could be, and he had long thought that she knew more of him than he at first suspected.

But whether it was so or not, he marvelled at the shrewd insight into his life which she had evidently possessed.

So he bade his friends adieu for a day or two, and journeyed down to the old Heath.

They were driven in an open carriage from the train to within a short distance of the sea, and near the spot where the old woman used to be seen wandering.

She was not in sight, nor any living being.

Hal remembered the old shelter she used to occupy, and resolved to go thither. Possibly she might be there, but he half feared he would not find her alive.

They walked by the beach and noted every peculiar rock and cranny until they were within a few yards of the old woman's retreat.

It was down in a small cleft in the cliff, the poorest form of hut, and in some eyes would have not been at all worthy of the name of shelter.

Hal remembered it, and as he was about to turn from the beach into the recess where it was, he saw a dark heap of something like a prostrate human being a short distance higher up the beach.

It lay close under the lea of a rock, and he thought he saw it move.

As he hurried forward, followed by Grip, he was startled to see the head rise and fall again.

It was something alive, and that something was the weird prophetess, who had by some occult power dipped into his future. Hal hurried up, intending to raise her, but with an effort she sat up.

"At last," she said, in feeble, broken tones, "you are here. I have hoped—longed—prayed for it. It does these old eyes of mine good to see you."

"You are ill," said Hal; "let me help you. I have a carriage not far away. Grip, go and fetch it."

"Stay! Not for me," she gasped; "I am no fit creature for a carriage, and, besides, all is over. I have fought and warded it off, but grim Death has won at las' Hal, listen to me. You remember our parting?"

"Well," he said.

"I kissed your forehead then," she said; "kiss mine now. Touch it ever so lightly with your lips, and receive a dying woman's blessing."

Neither rags, nor age, nor the seal of poverty and woe had robbed her of an indefinable something which told that she had once been a woman of breeding and beauty.

But Hal thought not of that. Without any sense of repugnance, he bent down and kissed her forehead.

————

CHAPTER XXXII.

FINALE.

"OH! pride and glory of the Warringtons, as you will be," said the weird creature. "Restorer of a dishonoured name—look into my eyes, so that I may see the light of true manhood in yours. Hal, do you remember the story of your great-grandfather, who had a sister —a wild Warrington?"

"I have heard it," Hal said, with a sudden quickening of his pulse.

"She was wilful—no more," said the dying woman. "The hot blood of her race ran fiercely in her veins. Hal, she loved—one who was a foe to our house—she fled with him—and was cast off. They never knew what became of her, never heard of her again ; but—oh ! can you not guess? I am very, very old—Hal—think?"

"Is it possible," Hal exclaimed, "that you—'

"Yes, I—the woman whom they cast off," she said "and on my way abroad with my husband—I loved him Hal—was wrecked on this coast. He was drowned—I survived—and here I have lived ever since. When they cast me off I vowed that I would never return, and I never did—I made no sign until now. Oh ! Hal, when first I saw you here—my heart yearned to my kith and kin—a love long still within my bosom was aroused. How have I thought of you since you went away."

She held his hand in hers, and, bending her face over it, a few hot tears fell—the last she was ever to shed.

"In a few minutes," she said, "all will be over—I shall be dead. But give me no better grave than my loved husband has—I must lie beside him, and give me no monument but the plain wooden emblem of suffering—a cross. Oh ! Hal—Hal—again touch my time-scarred and weather-beaten brow with your lips. The light of Heaven rest upon you—farewell ! Dark—all—darker—husband, I—"

She stopped short, raised herself a little higher, stared wildly about her for a moment, and fell back dead.

Hal did not leave the heath, or rather its neighbourhood, until he had fulfilled the last request of his aged relative.

At first there was some difficulty with the authorities about her interment ; but it was a lonely place, and the grave would not be unsightly to the eye.

Money smoothed the way, and then husband and wife were laid side by side.

Hal did not place a wooden cross there, but a marble one—a monument to the faithfulness of a woman who, if she erred in one thing, was wondrously true to the noblest instincts of her sex in another.

That she should die almost immediately they met seemed strange at first; but when he came to reflect he saw that she had been waiting for him—gifted, as it seemed, with a power to know that he was coming.

If he had been delayed, she would, perhaps, have held on.

Seeing him, which was all she desired, and, that fulfilled, she collapsed, which was no marvel, for she was very, very old.

And now Hal's path was almost clear.

He returned to town, and preparations were made for his marriage with Clara, which was, by the desire of both, to be a quiet one.

For all that, the big people would not let him rest.

They found him out, and made much of him and Clara and her friends.

If they had desired it, they could have had a surfeit of good society,

The wedding-day was fixed, and in a fortnight Hal and Clara would be made one, when it became known that the old Warrington estate was in the market.

Hal's solicitors went to work, and in an undemonstrative way secured it for him at a fair price.

Thus the old house became Hal's, and the future of the Warringtons was in his hands.

He went down to the old hall two days before his wedding, and looked over it prior to its being put into the hands of a builder to repair.

It had been sadly neglected, and looked quite forlorn.

"But by-and-bye, sir," said Grip, "there will be light and life in the old house again."

"It won't be my fault if it is not so," Hal replied.

And light and life came back to the old place—first with a happy husband and his fair young bride, then with little ones to raise musical echoes with their little feet in the old place.

The world ignored the past, and lived only in their present.

In Hal they saw what a Warrington could be, and shut their eyes to what a wild Warrington had been.

Felix and his father lived in London, for the most part, for Felix had received a very good appointment from one of Hal's friends.

But in a few years the old man died, then Felix married, and became a happy father too.

For Grip—for all—there was joy, and it was, as the old, faithful servitor used to say—

"Worth going through a lot of trouble to fully enjoy such a happy time."

It was, indeed.

After the clouds comes sunshine, and when the storm is past the holy calm arrives to give us rest,

THE END,

Printed by

Sully and Ford,

Plough Court,

Fetter Lane,

London.